COUNTRY
LEGACY

P9-EDI-226

COUNTRY LEGACY

THE HARD-TO-GET COWBOY

Crystal Green

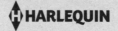

Special thanks and acknowledgment are given to
Crystal Green for her contribution to the
Montana Mavericks: The Texans Are Coming! continuity.

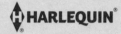

Recycling programs
for this product may
not exist in your area.

ISBN-13: 978-1-335-52346-4

The Hard-to-Get Cowboy
First published in 2011. This edition published in 2022.
Copyright © 2011 by Harlequin Enterprises ULC

For questions and comments about the quality of this book,
please contact us at CustomerService@Harlequin.com.

Harlequin Enterprises ULC
22 Adelaide St. West, 41st Floor
Toronto, Ontario M5H 4E3, Canada
www.Harlequin.com

Printed in U.S.A.

Crystal Green lives near Las Vegas and has written for Harlequin Special Edition and Harlequin Blaze. She loves to read, overanalyze movies and TV programs, practice yoga and travel when she can. You can read more about her at crystal-green.com.

To my beautiful, caring, hardworking mom—
you are the treasure of the family and we value
you beyond measure. Love you so much.

Prologue

Laila Cates stood on the stage in front of the cheering crowd, dressed in a white evening gown and a blue sash while holding a fresh bouquet of celebratory flowers.

"A five-time winner!" said the master of ceremonies, whose voice rang through the tent where the pageant was being held. "Give it up for Laila Cates for taking yet *another* Miss Frontier Days title!"

She touched the crown on her head. It'd been a long time since she'd been up here. Seven years since she'd stopped entering the pageant, seven years since she'd wanted to be known for more than what was on the outside.

But this year she'd come back to prove a point to Thunder Canyon.

Scanning the crowd, she saw the happy faces of the neighbors and friends she'd grown up with. People she worked with at the Thunder Canyon First Fidelity Bank, day in and day out. Her best friend, Dana, who'd entered Laila into the pageant without Laila even knowing it, clapped harder than anyone else.

She'd been the one who'd dared her to prove a point to the town, and Laila had taken her up on it, singing a song during the talent competition that emphasized a woman's hard work in this world and the accomplishments all of them could celebrate as they grew older.

And the judges had clearly appreciated it, recognizing that every year that passed by for a woman could be a plus rather than a negative.

After the noise subsided, Laila went to the microphone, shaking her head. "So I'm twenty-nine going on thirty. The jump to a new decade seems to be a big deal in most women's lives. We're supposed to be leaving behind our best, most youthful years, and truthfully, I've been a little nervous about that. I mean, this is when we get wrinkles, right? This is when our looks begin to fade." She smiled again. "Well, that's why I decided to compete in the pageant this year, to see if any of that mattered when it comes right down to it."

A few hoots, hollers.

She went on. "You all have shown tonight that age and life experience are important— that they add to who we are and how others see us. And, even though this is definitely my last time competing for the title, I'm looking forward to a new win each year, except not on a stage. In life. In *everything*."

Another round of applause, and Laila gave a jaunty little salute to the crowd, ready to give up the stage to all the other women who wanted to show Thunder Canyon what they had to offer—no matter what their age—in the future.

That was when the audience parted to let through a strapping, broad-shouldered man with blond hair.

At first, Laila thought he was merely there to offer congratulations. It was Hollis Cade Pritchett, the man she'd been seeing on and off for years on a casual basis. Cade, as he was known to just about everyone but his sister and her husband, accepted what Laila had professed all along—that she never wanted to get married—and that had apparently suited him just fine.

Until now, it seemed.

"Marry me, Laila," he said loudly.

As his deep voice carried, Laila blinked, then put her hand over the mic. The device whimpered with feedback as a wave of silence traveled over the audience.

This wasn't like Cade, to be joking around. And she suspected that it *was* a joke, because he was acting...different. Heck, she could even say that the normally levelheaded woodworker might've even tipped back a few beers, judging by the high flush on his cheeks. But Cade wasn't a big drinker.

So what explained the intensity in his gaze?

His brother, Dean, broke out of the crowd and stood by Cade, wearing a tight grin and slapping him on the back, buddy-style.

"Don't listen to him, Laila," the youngest Pritchett boy said. "*I'm* the one you should marry!"

Okay—now it was pretty obvious from the way Dean slightly slurred that they *had* been indulging for some odd reason. Like his brother, Dean was the strong, silent type, hardly prone to tomfoolery like this.

By now, the crowd had broken into a chorus of laughter, urging the Pritchetts on.

Laila kept her composure, as well as her sense of humor. This was starting to feel like a circus act, but maybe she'd only encouraged that by competing in the pageant at this age when it was supposed to be a young girls' competition.

She would take her knocks, because using a pageant title to make a statement about inner beauty was loaded with irony, and not everyone was going to get it.

It was just another idea some of the townsfolk probably wouldn't take seriously from her.

Just then, another man came to the front of the stage—a guy who wasn't as familiar to Laila, even though she knew darn well who he was.

Who didn't?

Tall, lean and roguish in his jeans, boots and black Western shirt, Jackson Traub was new in town—one of the Texans who'd come to Thunder Canyon to develop his family's oil shale business.

And he was also known to be a troublemaker who'd caused a wild ruckus at his own brother's wedding reception several months ago.

Was he about to stir things up here, too, just for the heck of it?

Just because rumor had it that he enjoyed raising Cain?

Laila should've been sending him a "Don't you dare do it" glare, but…

But just look at him.

She was too busy taking in a deep breath, feeling a burst of tingles as they rolled through every single inch of her while he grinned up at her on the stage.

Lord help her, but a bad-boy reputation did something to a girl who'd spent her life doing everything right.

He swept off his hat and held it over his heart while raising his own voice over the crowd's. "Neither of these boys is worthy. *I'm* going to marry the lovely Laila!"

Something primal hit her in the belly, and hard.

But it had nothing to do with the ridiculous proposal. Nothing at all.

It was only that his brown hair had been tousled so carelessly by the removal of his hat, and even from the stage, Laila could see the glint in his dust-devil brown gaze as he looked up at her and grinned even wider.

In spite of everything, she grinned right back,

though hers was of the sweet/sarcastic variety. No one was going to make a complete mockery out of this night.

And no one—not even a slick Texan—was going to make it all better with a naughty smile and a joke, either.

Jackson Traub lifted an eyebrow, as if appreciating her feisty look.

As if challenged by it.

It took some effort to drag her gaze away from him—my, did it ever—but she turned her attention back to the audience while their laughter died down.

"See?" she said. "Here's proof that life really doesn't end after your twenties, girls. Everything improves with age, including the amount of attention."

As cheers erupted, she waited for silence before continuing.

"But you all know that my heart belongs to Thunder Canyon. And, for all you fellas out there who'd planned to offer more proposals, you know I adore every last one of you, but I must tell you once and for all that I. Am. Never. Getting. Married. Life's too short!"

As the place went nuts, she winked at the crowd, then smiled at the Pritchett brothers, telling them that there were no hard feelings about their ill-timed shenanigans.

Dean was glancing at his brother, as if to gauge Cade's reaction.

And what Laila saw in Cade almost chipped away at her heart.

It seemed as if he'd just been kicked in the gut, his face ruddy, his hands fisted at his sides.

Oh, God. *Had* he been serious about proposing?

No way—not when she'd been very clear over the years how she felt about settling down. Not Cade Pritchett—a man who never impulsively shouted out things like proposals in front of a hundred other people.

Without a word, he turned to leave, his shoulders stiff, and Dean followed him, leaving the third suitor behind.

As Laila met the amused gaze of Jackson Traub, the last man standing, he put his hat back on, then touched the brim. The gesture might've been a touché from someone who clearly appreciated her firm stance on singlehood. Word had it that he'd even caused that scene at his brother's reception because he was the ultimate bachelor, and he was intent on swearing off matrimony himself. It was just that he hadn't exactly been speaking to a sympathetic audience at a *wedding,* for heaven's sake.

Before he turned around and disappeared into the crowd, he sent Laila one last wicked grin.

Then he was gone, leaving her with a burning yen to see him again, for better...

Or for worse.

Chapter 1

Nearly a week later, Laila sat at a corner table in the bar section at the Hitching Post, keeping her eye on the entrance as she traced the sweat off the mug of a lemonade she hadn't touched.

She'd been playing phone tag with Cade, and they'd finally agreed to meet here tonight, among the after-work crowd enjoying Happy Hour in this rumored former house of ill repute that'd been turned into a bar and grill.

She tried to ignore the line of ranch hands at the bar—the men who kept glancing over and peering at her from beneath the shade of their hats. One in particular, Duncan Brooks, who worked on Mayor Bo Clifton's spread, was trying to catch Laila's attention.

Then again, he always was, and she wished he wouldn't do that. The mustached, stocky cowboy was forever looking at her with that moony gaze men sometimes got when they were around Laila—that struck-by-a-beauty-queen gander that made her wish she had set out to clear up everyone's perceptions of her from the very first time she'd been old enough to date.

With a polite nod to Duncan—nothing more, nothing to encourage him—she took a sip of her lemonade and shifted her attention to the painting over the bar. It featured the Shady Lady herself, Lily Divine, draped in diaphanous material, wearing a mysterious smile. Long before Thunder Canyon had experienced its recent gold rush and the place had moved from a sleepy spot on the map to a boomtown with a resort that attracted the rich and adventurous alike, and long before the town had undergone an economic fall that they were still recovering from, Lily had been a woman of questionable morals. A supposed heartbreaker.

Was that what Cade thought about Laila now, after she'd shot him down at the pageant?

Was that why he hadn't been returning her calls?

She would soon see, because he was just now walking through the entrance, pausing to glance around for Laila.

She waved a tentative hello, and his hands fisted by his sides, just as they had the night of the pageant. He walked toward her in his sheepskin jacket—a necessity now that the weather had finally turned from Indian summer to October cool.

Laila held back a frown. It was tough to see Cade Pritchett in such a state. He was a hardy man, a local hero who'd played down his part in rescuing a young girl from drowning in Silver Stallion Lake about a year ago. Naturally, he'd refused any accolades.

He was the best of guys. The best of friends—until recently.

She'd already ordered a soda for him, and as he doffed his jacket, tossed it over the back of a chair, then sat, she pushed the beverage toward him as if it were a peace offering.

"I wasn't so sure you'd come here tonight," she said.

Cade didn't utter a word. After years of dating him—never serious enough to have gotten totally intimate with him, though—Laila nevertheless knew enough about Cade to realize that he was weighing whatever he was thinking carefully before saying it.

She also knew that when he spoke, it would be in a low voice that would give most any girl delicious shivers and, not for the first time, Laila wondered just why it didn't affect *her* like that.

What was wrong with her that she didn't feel *that* way about him…or about anybody, much, except for a couple of men who'd seemed like Mr. Rights until they'd proven to be Mr. Maybe-Not-After-Alls?

A flash of roguish brown eyes and an equally devastating grin flew across her mind's eye, but she quashed all thoughts of Jackson Traub.

He certainly wasn't her type, and she'd been reminding herself of that all week.

Cade met her gaze head-on. "I've been doing a lot of thinking lately, and what I have to say to you now isn't impulsive or ill-considered. I've even been thinking about what I came here to tell you long *before* the pageant."

She didn't like how this was starting. "I'm not sure I know what you're talking about."

"The future, Laila."

His direct manner made her wary.

"You're not the only one who's entered a

new phase of life," he said. "When a person gets older, he starts to reassess where he's been. Where he's going."

His blue gaze was so intense that Laila prayed he wasn't about to say what she thought he was going to say...

But he went and said it, anyway.

"I wasn't fooling around when I asked you to marry me."

She tried not to react, even though it felt as if a shadow had steamrolled her. "Cade, I didn't mean to embarrass you by turning you down so publicly, but you know how I feel about marriage."

"I know how you always *said* you feel."

Now Laila was really confused. Had she been sending Cade mixed signals or something? But that couldn't be the case. She'd always been *very* clear on her feelings about staying single.

"Cade..." she said softly just before he interrupted her.

"Just listen... I know full well that you're not in love with me. But we have a lot to offer each other in spite of that."

He paused, and she searched his gaze, seeing that there was something deep going on in this man. Sadly, she even wondered if this had anything to do with how Cade had lost the woman he'd wanted to marry to an early death years ago.

Maybe that was why Laila had been drawn to him, as a companion more than anything else. He had shut down emotionally after his lover's passing, and he'd probably seen in Laila a person who didn't get involved much with heavy emotions herself.

Did he think that she would never expect more out of him than he was capable of giving after having his heart broken?

The realization left her a bit hollow. It wasn't that she couldn't love anyone, it was just that she'd always thought of herself as a career woman—one who'd worked her tail off to become branch manager of the bank. One who, admittedly, loved to flirt and play the field to a certain point.

At her silence, he had straightened up in his chair, as if thinking that she was actually considering his point. He seemed so confident now that a scratch of pain scored her.

"Right before the pageant," he said, "I had a good long talk with my brothers."

"And with your other friend, Jack Daniels?"

Cade's skin went ruddy. "All right. A little whiskey was involved, and the more I had, the more I decided I wanted to get an answer from you once and for all about where we were headed. And I don't regret bringing this up, Laila, not even in such a spectacular fashion. Not even if I made a donkey of myself at the pageant and my own brother took enough pity on me to propose, too, turning my folly into a joke everyone could laugh off."

What she needed was for a hole to open up in the ceiling that would suck her right into it and out of this discussion. "I—"

"I need to finish what I came here to say."

He'd raised his voice and, from the corner of her gaze, she saw Duncan Brooks stand away from the bar, obviously hearing Cade and not liking his tone one bit. Laila sent a reassuring smile at the ranch hand, letting him know everything was okay.

Appeased, Duncan went back to drinking his beer, hunched over it as he leaned on the bar.

"I'm tired of being alone," Cade said. "Aren't you?"

She sighed, hating that she would have to be terribly blunt. "No."

He frowned.

"Why does that surprise you?" she asked. "You know I love my life. I love going home to my apartment every night and eating what I want to eat, when I want to eat it. I love watching what I want to watch on TV…"

"You don't ever get lonely? You never wake up at night in your empty bed and wonder if it's always going to be that way?"

She didn't know what to say, because there *were* times when that exact thing happened— shadows on the pale walls, the inexplicable sense that she was genuinely alone.

But then she would go right back to sleep, waking up to a new day, loving her life all over again, even as an itch of loneliness remained in the back of her mind….

Still, there were good reasons she was never going to get married, and the biggest one was because of what she'd seen in her mom. Laila's mother had tried her best not to show how life had let her down. Even though Mom loved all six of her children, Laila had seen how she had ordered college catalogues and paged through them with a slight, sad smile at the kitchen table after she thought all the kids were in bed. She'd heard Mom say on more than one occasion that she should've taken her studies more seriously and that Laila shouldn't ever rely on her looks when she had such a brain.

And she also knew that Mom had settled down young.

Too young?

Always wondering, never having the courage to ask, Laila had promised herself that *she* would give life a chance before getting serious with anyone, and she was damn happy with her decision as it stood.

Right?

She pushed aside her drink and rested her elbows on the table. "Loneliness is no reason to get married, Cade."

His jaw hardened as he surveyed her. Then, hardly swayed, he said, "We can learn to love each other... I can even give you children before it's too late."

Oof.

That really got her. But she wasn't sure why Cade's words smarted the way they did.

Had she been thinking about her future lately, even beyond wrinkles, in a more profound way than she even admitted to herself? And, heck...

She even wondered if she'd actually entered the Miss Frontier Days pageant for the final time because she'd needed some kind of reassurance that she *was* still young enough to be desirable, that she didn't need to change her life and get validation from marriage or kids...

Her throat felt tender as she tried to swallow. She didn't like what she was thinking, and she wouldn't let Cade's words bother her. But how could she tell him that she didn't feel more for him than companionship?

Just as she was wishing again for that hole to open up in the ceiling, there was a stir in the Hitching Post as someone sauntered inside.

As soon as she saw Jackson Traub bellying up to the bar in a dark brushed-twill coat with his Stetson pulled low over his brow, her body flared with heat.

Star-spangly, popping, sizzling heat.

Something she *definitely* didn't feel for Cade.

She must've been staring, and Jackson Traub must've felt it, because as he ordered a drink from the bartender, he pushed back his hat so she could see his brown gaze locking onto hers.

Her heart seemed to shoot down to her belly, where it revolved, sending the rest of her topsy-turvy, too.

She expected him to give her one of those grins he was so good at, expected him to maybe even wink as a reminder of the night he'd lightheartedly proposed like a scoundrel come out of nowhere.

But he only turned back to the bartender as the man slid a glass of what looked to be straight-up whiskey to him.

Jackson Traub scooped it right up, then downed it before ordering another, ignoring Laila as if nothing had ever passed between them.

Baffled, she stared down at the table.

Was he ignoring her?

Or could it be that he really didn't remember their "moment" at the pageant?

Or maybe there just hadn't been a "moment" for him…

Rascal. He was truly making her wonder. But let him play his games. She'd been dating since sixteen, when her parents had finally allowed it after she'd blossomed early. She had a pretty good sense of when a man was interested or not.

Still, she peered over at Jackson Traub again, just to see if he was looking.

He wasn't.

"Laila?" Cade asked.

He sounded offended that she'd mentally wandered from the conversation. In fact, he was looking more intense than ever—so much so that Laila sank into her chair, wishing fervently, once again, for that hole in the ceiling to appear, suck her up and take her away from all the truths Cade was making her face tonight.

Jackson was a patient man.

He was also mildly perceptive, if he did say so himself, and he knew when a woman—even a cool beauty queen like Laila Cates—was aware of his presence.

As he nursed his second whiskey, he nodded to the man at the end of the bar, an acquaintance Jackson had met during his short time here. Woody Paulson, the manager of LipSmackin' Ribs, a joint that didn't so much compete with the rib restaurant of Jackson's cousin, DJ, as stay in its shadow.

Woody nodded back to Jackson, but the interaction didn't take his mind off Laila. He wondered if she was still watching him, yet he refrained from taking a peek. Instead, he imagined her in that white evening gown, the first time he'd seen the infamous Thunder Canyon beauty in person, on the stage, her long, wavy blond hair silky under the crown she wore, her blue eyes bright, her skin smooth and pale as cream.

A challenge if he ever met one.

A woman he wanted with every beat of his pulse.

He hadn't initially come to Thunder Canyon for a good time, though. Months ago, it'd been his brother Corey's wedding that had brought him here, and Jackson had stayed just long enough to throw a few punches during the reception before returning to his gentleman's ranch in Midland, Texas, then back to work for the family oil business, where he spent the weekdays in his city penthouse.

During the past few months, he'd been thinking hard about the mess he'd created up here in Montana during Corey's nuptials. At first, Jackson had chalked it all up to just being a bad day, and he'd had a few too many champagnes as well as a few too many thoughts about how his brothers seemed to be falling prey to marriage, an institution that Jackson had never cottoned to.

So he'd spoken his mind at the reception, saying that matrimony was a great way to ruin a relationship. And, as if *that* wasn't awful enough, he'd gone on to pretty much call his two married brothers wusses.

He'd said that *he* would never change his life for a woman, and he'd damn well meant it.

Needless to say, the brothers Traub hadn't taken kindly to his opinions, and Jackson had left Thunder Canyon with his fists and face bruised, knowing that he'd gone too far. But he'd tried his best during his time away to think on how he was going to make it up to his family.

Not only that—he'd really taken a good look at what he had or hadn't accomplished during his thirty-four years here on earth, and he didn't like the view much at all.

That's why, when his older brother Ethan stepped up his attempts to explore oil shale extraction opportunities, Jackson saw an opportunity not only to get into his family's good graces again, but...

Hell. In spite of his shortcomings, he loved his family more than anything, and he just wanted to make them see that he wasn't a loser who would always start fistfights at weddings. The superficial guy who could be so much more than the company "schmoozer" who closed deals and wooed clients.

So here he was, back in Thunder Canyon, convinced that he could finally put what brains he had to some use in getting this new branch of Traub Oil Industries started. He'd actually persuaded his brother, Ethan, that he could head up community outreach and education, since Traub Oil Montana was exploring new, more environmentally friendly ways of extraction at the Bakken Shale; he would also be working with the ranchers and landowners from whom the company had bought or leased rights.

Even though Jackson wasn't here for the long run, he was going to make his time in Thunder Canyon matter, but that didn't mean he couldn't use a little entertainment while he was around....

He finally took a sidelong glance at Laila Cates, but she'd gone back to her conversation with Cade Pritchett, whom Jackson only knew because of his outburst at the pageant. Honestly, Jackson had felt for the man after he'd shouted out that proposal. In fact, after Cade's brother had come to his rescue with another marriage offer to Laila, Jackson had impulsively broken in with his own. It wasn't so much for Cade's sake as Laila's because, even under her unruffled façade, Jackson had sensed how vexed Laila had seemed on that stage, and if there was one thing Jackson was, it was a sucker for a woman, especially one who seemed embarrassed that her big night had been shot to hell by an unexpected profession of devotion.

He was pretty sure that someone like Laila was used to men falling all over her, although not in such a mortifyingly public way.

And he wasn't about to be like the other guys.

At present, as Laila sat there looking as uncomfortable as all get out once again, Jackson could tell she was in another tight spot, that here was a woman who was just about telepathically asking anyone in the room to interrupt the conversation she was having.

Now it wasn't as if Jackson would've done what he did next if Laila hadn't been providing a clear opening for him. If she was having a grand old time with her date, he would've stayed a mile away from her.

But being the woman-loving sucker he was, he turned from the bar, getting an even better look at her. His heartbeat picked up.

She was dressed as if she'd just come from work, in a stylish dark gray pinstriped suit, and her wavy mass of blond hair—shiny and silky enough to make his fingers itch to touch it—was swept up in a style that left some strands framing her face.

And…that face.

It belonged to a beauty queen, all right. High cheekbones, full red lips, long black lashes, delicate eyebrows and all.

Now it was more than his heart that was thudding.

To rescue her again or not to rescue her?

There wasn't much of a choice, and he left his whiskey glass at the bar as he crossed the floor.

She seemed to know he was coming before he even got there, and that did something to him—riled him up inside, stretched a string of lit firecrackers through him.

"Well," he said as she parted her lips, as if to utter something before he beat her to it. "If it isn't my bride-to-be."

Okay, there it was. If she gave any indication that he was intruding, he would go.

He even gave her another chance to shoo him off. "I didn't mean to interrupt anything—"

Cade and Laila spoke at the same time.

"You are," the man said.

"You're not," she said.

Jackson had sure called it correctly. And when Laila nudged a chair away from the table with her foot, she only emphasized the point.

Had Cade proposed again to this woman

who'd announced to the whole town that she *Never. Wanted. To. Get. Married?*

Was that why she looked like a deer caught in the headlights?

Cade had seen her pushing out the chair, too, but Jackson only tipped his hat to them both, then took a seat, signaling to a waitress who came right over, all smiles.

"What can I do you for?" she asked.

"A round of beers," Jackson said. "On my tab."

When she scuttled off, she left a view of the bar, and Jackson couldn't help but notice that many a male gaze was turned his way, obviously envious that he was sitting at Laila's table. One man in particular—a cowboy with a chunky silver belt buckle and a mustache— watched Jackson for a moment too long before looking away.

Cade's voice rumbled. "Not tonight, Traub."

Jackson was checking in with Laila, whose smile was forced, even though it seemed to be asking him to stay, no matter what.

Sure enough.

When Jackson faced Cade, the man seemed likely to wring his neck, if the sight of his bunched fists on the tabletop meant anything.

Time for some peace talk. "Just introducing

myself around town." He stuck out his hand for a shake. "You can call me Jackson."

"I know who you are." Cade shot Laila a glance, and if it could speak, it would've said, *You gonna do anything to get him out of here or should I?*

But when Laila only took a sip of the lemonade that had been waiting in front of her all this time, Cade stood, got out his wallet, then tossed some bills on the table.

When he spoke, it was to Laila, and it was far quieter than Jackson expected.

"Just think about what I said."

Then he was gone, leaving only the background murmur of bar discussion over the strains of Merle Haggard on the jukebox.

The waitress came with the beers, and Jackson decided that if Cade wouldn't be around to drink his, he would gladly do the honors.

He didn't make anything out of the sassy smile that the waitress gave him, instead taking a swig of his drink, then leaning back in his chair and grinning at Laila.

There was a little beauty mark near the tip of her mouth, and he wished she would smile, just as prettily as she had on that stage last week. But he was out of luck. She only traced a pattern on the table from the condensation that had dropped down from the lemonade mug.

"Was I in the wrong when I sat down here?" Jackson asked.

"No, you weren't. Thank you. It was one of those discussions. You know—the kind that you don't want to have in the middle of a bar?"

"Glad to have been of assistance."

She sighed, still tracing pictures on the table. Jackson couldn't make hide nor hair of what she was drawing.

"If he puts the moves on you again," he said, meaning to cheer her up, "you just give a holler. He's big, but I can take him."

There it was—a wisp of a smile now.

"Truly," he added. "I know how to dodge and weave. Also, I've got a twin back home who's always willing to stand up for a lady, too."

"Good heavens—there's more than one of you?"

He chuckled. "I'm afraid so." Getting even more comfortable, he propped his booted ankle just above his knee. "But Jason's far less reckless. That's what everyone says, anyway."

"I'd heard you're a rebel, even before you showed up at the pageant to cause mischief."

He took that in stride. "Heard from who?"

She had a flush on her cheeks, and it looked so sweet that Jackson's veins tangled.

"I'd heard," she said, "just in general. Thunder Canyon's a small town, so gossip travels."

"I know. That's why I proposed to you, Miss Laila—because *I'd* heard you were the perfect woman for me."

Her gaze widened.

He laughed. "You don't have to say it again—the part about your never getting married. The message came through loud and clear at the pageant."

She blew out a breath, as if she'd been dreading having to repeat it to yet another suitor. It made him think that Cade's pageant proposal had been much more than just an impetuous moment, that it bothered her far more than she'd let on in public.

That she was just as determinedly single as he was?

"I happen to agree 100 percent with you about the holy state of matrimony," he said. "I'm not sure what the appeal is."

"Ask your brothers, Corey and Dillon. I'm sure they can wax on about it."

"No, thanks. It's bad enough that Ethan just got engaged, too. I never thought I'd see him strapping himself to a ball and chain. All I can do now is hope that Jason and my sister, Rose, stick with me."

"You talk as if the rest of your family has abandoned you or something."

He paused. He'd never thought of it that way before, but that's what he'd been feeling during Corey's wedding—abandonment. Being left behind while everyone else traveled ahead to what were supposed to be bigger and better things in life.

She seemed to realize that she'd hit some kind of target on him, whether he'd meant to show it or not.

"Or maybe you're just a born rebel," she said. "I could tell the minute you jumped into the fray at the pageant that your skills were instinctive."

"Hey, I was only trying to ease a tense situation." He shrugged. "And maybe have a little fun."

"I rest my case."

He picked up his mug, toasted her with it, then drank.

When he was done, she was watching him, her bluebonnet eyes narrowed just the slightest bit, as if she was turning over a million questions about him in her head.

If she was sitting there wondering what went

into the creation of a rebel like him, he wasn't about to give her answers.

He wanted to get back to the flirtation. He hadn't met anyone in Thunder Canyon who'd made him forget all the tough questions that had been echoing in his brain ever since the wedding brawl, and he wasn't about to lead her into thinking that he was the kind of guy who was even comfortable having that type of conversation.

Leaning his elbows on the table, he sent Laila his most lethal grin.

"If you're thinking of asking me questions, don't."

"Questions about what?"

"Serious stuff. The kind of questions that come after a first date."

She laughed, as if he'd stepped over a line she'd already drawn with him. "Are you saying this is a date?"

"Nope." He lowered his voice. "But when we do go on our first one, I'm just laying out some ground rules. I don't want to hear any of the kind of questions that make you narrow your eyes like that."

She was flustered, and he hadn't expected that from a graceful, composed woman like Laila Cates.

"When we...?"

"When we go on our first date," he said, completing her sentence, enjoying the hell out of the chase.

Because he always got what he wanted when it came to women, and Laila Cates wouldn't be an exception.

"I never said I would—"

"You didn't have to, Miss Laila. But you know damn well that we're going to go out." He lifted an eyebrow. "It's just a matter of when."

Chapter 2

He sure was cocky, Laila thought, her pulse racing so fast that it felt as if she was running.

Jackson Traub—arrogant and altogether too confident.

And they were talking about a date.

Her. *Him*.

She could just imagine what her parents—no, the whole town—might say if they caught wind of this conversation. Laila Cates, the proper bank manager, the woman who did everything according to the letter, hanging around with a rabble-rousing Texas stranger.

But then a different type of thought altogether started to take shape in her mind….

What if going on a date with a fly-by-night man like Jackson Traub could convince Cade Pritchett that she really *wasn't* longing for stability and marriage?

Suddenly, she liked the whole idea. Especially since, even if she *wasn't* looking to settle down, there would be no future with Jackson, anyway. Because the talk around Thunder Canyon was that he was merely here to work on that oil shale project.

Here and gone.

There was an appeal to that. And there was a definite appeal to *him,* too, as he sat across from her with that crooked grin, all playful cowboy, the complete opposite of a man like Cade.

What would be the harm in just one date?

But then something went swirly in her belly, melty and hot, trickling downward until it settled in the core of her.

She shoved the sensation aside.

"Come on, Laila," Jackson said, his brown eyes glinting with that flirtiness she'd seen before. "I'm just talking about a date, not a marriage proposal."

Wasn't he a card.

Or, more to the point, a wild card.

"Very funny," she said.

"Don't tell me a man doesn't have a chance with you." He sent a glance over his shoulder, toward the door where Cade had disappeared only moments ago. "Or maybe there's something else to it."

She had the feeling he was going to go somewhere she didn't want to go.

"Maybe," he said, "there really is something between you and Pritchett, even if you were desperate to get away from him less than five minutes ago."

Jackson said it in a teasing way, as if he didn't believe it for a second.

Was there anything this Texan didn't see? It was as if he could read her through and through.

Yet she refused to dignify his question with an answer. She knew when a troublemaker was stirring it up.

He chuckled, just as the jukebox went silent, leaving only the laughter from the bar patrons.

She crossed her arms over her chest.

"We both know that there's no way you'll end up with a nice guy like Pritchett." He put the glass to his lips, drinking.

His throat worked with every swallow.

She couldn't take her eyes off him, couldn't stop herself from thinking what it would feel like to have her lips against that throat, the warm skin roughened by stubble from a five o'clock shadow.

But she managed to pull her gaze away before she offered evidence that he was right about her being attracted to a bad boy over a good one.

"I may not end up with Cade," she said, "but that doesn't mean I'd put myself in the position of ending up anywhere with you."

He put down the drained mug. "Shot through the heart, Miss Laila. You've got some excellent aim."

"And *you* don't know enough about me to go around predicting who's my type and who's not."

"I can sure guess." He sat back in his chair, long-limbed and laconic.

A wise girl would have gotten up from the table by now, heading through the door for home, where it would be safe. But here she was flirting with him.

And she didn't want to stop.

He said, "I surmise that, all your life, you've dated men who are steady. Men who drive just five miles above the speed limit—and that's their idea of living dangerously. And yours, too."

He didn't even seem to be expecting a response—not judging by the long, cocky stare he was fixing on her, one that suggested he knew how madly her blood was flying through her veins, just from being near him.

When had she ever felt like this before?

Was it curiosity that was keeping her here? Or was it because the big 3-0 was looming above her like a net, ready to drop and wrap her up in the great unknown?

Whatever it was, she finally, quietly dared to say, "And just what would a man like you have to offer on a…date?"

Jackson lowered his ankle from where it'd been resting on his knee. "I drive a whole lot faster than the speed limit, for one thing."

"And you'll be driving just as fast out of town, once you're done with your business here."

"So I will. But a woman who doesn't aim to settle down wouldn't care so much about my leaving. We understand each other's philosophies on that."

Was he saying that they had something in common? That because she didn't have any plans to get married, she was just like him?

The notion should've disturbed her, but instead, it sent a shot of adrenaline racing through her body.

"Come on, Laila," he said, leaning toward

her even closer. Charmingly. Devastatingly. "One date. That's all I'm asking for."

She swallowed. "That's all?"

What was she doing?

"One date is all…for now." He stood to his full height, towering above her, then leaned down until his words brushed her ear with warmth. "But I'm pretty sure you'll find that one date won't be enough."

And, with that, he ambled away, not even bothering to get her phone number or arrange a time to pick her up.

Just as cocky—and tempting—as he'd been when he'd entered the bar.

"Seriously?" said Laila's best friend, Dana Hanson, while sitting in a chair by Laila's office desk the next day. "You're actually going out with that pugilist?"

Laila closed the glass door that separated her working space from the rest of the bank, which bustled with people during lunch hour. Dana, who was wearing her sandy hair in a conservative upswept style that artfully hid the purple streak she'd decided to add last weekend, had pushed her decorative Clark Kent glasses to the crown of her head in her awe of Laila's situation.

"I *think* I have a date with the pugilist," Laila said, staying near the door where she could keep an eye on things.

"How is it that you're not sure?"

"Well, he asked me out then just sort of... left me hanging."

"A proficient tease. He sounds like an all-around bad seed." Dana waggled her eyebrows. "*I* would go out with him, just for the adventure."

"I'm not sure I should, even though I kind of said I would." Laila shook her head. "He has me all confused."

"Then that's why you're into him. He's different. He's the guy who makes our straight-arrow golden girl feel like she could get a little tarnished. And he throws you for a loop when you don't normally get riled up by men." Dana pointed at her. "That's why you like him."

"Technically, I didn't say yes to a date."

"But you didn't refuse."

"I should've."

"Why?"

Laila gave up trying to make sense out of any of it, then motioned to the suit she was wearing—a black and white advertisement for dedicated businesswomen everywhere. "Because of this, Dane. Because maybe I'm a little..."

"Bored with it all?"

Nodding, Laila leaned her head against a wooden reinforcement by the door. All around, her office seemed so bland, with its chrome touches, the fake potted flowers in strategic places. Real ones would've been prettier, but it took commitment to maintain them.

"I know, life's rough," Dana said. "Every man wants the beauty queen. It must be a slog, fending them all off."

"You know what I mean by bored."

"Yeah. And I'd have some compassion if you weren't you."

She knew her friend didn't mean anything cruel by that; Laila had tried all her life not to be smug about her looks, appreciating what God had given her while always working for more.

"I have to say, though," Dana said, "that when the Pritchett boys and then this Traub fellow proposed at Miss Frontier Days, I did feel for you. I actually regretted entering you into the pageant...for about two minutes."

"No major harm done."

"So if he does take you out, where do you think it'll be?" Dana asked, not even remotely off the subject of Jackson. "Bowling? Cow-tipping in the fields?"

"Hilarious."

"You've totally been thinking about your choices."

Lying was futile, and Dana was smirking now.

"What?" Laila asked.

"You're fidgety about this. Laila Cates, I've never seen you so nervous, not even back in our junior year, when you had your very first date, with Gary Scott."

Nervous? Her?

Couldn't be.

Laila opened the door, smiling caustically at her friend. "Isn't it time for you to get back to the loan desk?"

Dana smoothed down her red skirt and headed for the exit. "You're affected, Laila. A-F-F-E-C-T-E-D."

And she left, still smirking.

Laila tried to get back to the paperwork on her desk, plus the million-and-one to-do items on her list, but she just couldn't focus on work. So it was almost a relief when she saw the bank's elderly owner, Mike Trudeau, walking by the windows of her office.

She'd been waiting for her boss to come in for hours and, even before she went to him, she marked him off her to-do list, then rose from her seat. With a smooth gait, she went outside, following him to his own office, which was decorated with a huntsman's touch, featuring kitschy, homey things like a mallard clock and a painting of buffalo roaming a prairie.

He was standing behind his desk, accessing his computer when she walked in.

"Morning, Laila."

Casual, friendly, with the silver hair of a grandpa... He shouldn't have intimidated Laila in the least, especially since he'd shown up to check in on his business dressed in jeans and a bulky sweater, just as laid-back as usual.

And, as usual, Laila put on the same façade that made everyone think that nothing ever got to her.

"Morning, Mike. Do you have a moment?"

"For our reigning Miss Frontier Days? Always."

He motioned toward the chair in front of his large oak desk, and she sat, crossing her legs, slipping a folder toward him.

"Ah," he said. "Do we have another idea today?"

She was used to this bit of harmless condescension in his tone, and she kept smiling, even if every idea she brought to him seemed to end up in the garbage heap. Or, more likely, she suspected that there was a vortex that could only be accessed through a drawer in his desk, and that was where her ideas went.

But that didn't stop her from trying again, especially since this particular idea was closer to her heart than usual.

"Yes, sir, I've got another one," she said, folding her hands in her lap.

He didn't make a move to open the folder, so she started her pitch, determined that he would at least hear it.

"It's no secret that most people in Thunder Canyon have been hit hard by the economy," she said, leaving out the fact that Mike Trudeau himself was flush right now, along with his bank.

"True enough." He was still fussing with his computer.

"And I know you've expressed an interest in getting this town back on its feet. You've been meeting with the mayor, along with other leading members of the community. I don't know how many ideas you've come up with, but if you'll take a look at some figures I've put together to support what I have in mind..."

Mr. Trudeau finally opened the folder, but his expression didn't change.

Laila cleared her throat. "I think the bank is in

a position to make more loans to struggling local homeowners and small businesses in Thunder Canyon and, as you'll see, I've proposed some avenues to do that, while benefiting our business in the long run."

"Interesting," he said, paging through the folder.

Laila couldn't stop looking at the top of his silver head, and when she realized that her fingers were clutching her skirt, she loosened her hold.

Mr. Trudeau closed the folder. "Looks like that college business degree did you some good, Laila."

"Thank you, sir."

"Beats getting an MRS degree, like the girls in my day used to do."

Laila kept her mouth shut. Even though she'd decided to major in business because she thought she should, rather than out of a love for the subject, she was proud of her accomplishments. So were her parents, who'd always emphasized a firm work ethic in their household.

Her boss sat in his chair with a sense of finality. "I'll go over it, Laila. Thanks for your work."

She almost said, "But…"

Yet she didn't, even if, so many times before, she'd heard Mike Trudeau use the same brush-off.

Sometimes, when she talked to him, she felt as if there was no substance in her at all. But maybe this time he would believe that there was more to her than what he saw—something she'd tried, and failed, to prove all too recently at Miss Frontier Days.

Holding back that frustration, she got up, thanking her boss again, then headed for the door.

She shut it behind her, adapting a pleasant expression for the customers who greeted her on their way to the tellers' windows.

In spite of what had just happened, as long as Laila could use her brain, she was going to *keep* putting proposals on her boss's desk. She would keep on fighting the good fight....

On her way across the tiled lobby, a woman's voice stopped her.

"Laila!"

She turned to find Jacey Weidemeyer, one of her friends from high school who patronized the bank. She was dressed in jeans and a thick sweater that almost hid the reminder of a recently pregnant belly.

And she was holding a baby.

For some reason, Laila's heart twisted at the sight of the newborn in Jacey's arms, an infant swaddled in a pink blanket with a tiny knit hat covering her head, her eyes closed in sleep, her skin smooth and rosy.

"Oh," Laila whispered. "She's beautiful."

Jacey stroked her daughter's cheek. "Meet Hannah. This is the first time we've gotten out of the house since I gave birth."

Laila touched the baby's little hand. Tiny nails. Tiny fingers.

Her heart seemed to sink inside her for some reason.

Jacey said, "We're going to have a reception in a few weeks. I'll email you an invitation."

"I'd…" What, love to go? It was the last thing Laila thought she would ever have said. She amended herself appropriately. "I'll be there."

After they finished chatting and Jacey left for the teller's window, Laila looked after her and Hannah, pangs invading her deep and low.

Was it because of what Cade had said last night about how he could give her children before it was too late?

Having no idea, Laila went back to her office, leaving the door slightly ajar behind her.

By the time a chilly, star-pinned night hushed over Thunder Canyon, Jackson had left the brick office building that his brother, Ethan, had established for Traub Oil Montana in Old Town and arrived at the Thunder Canyon Resort to meet some of his family for dinner at DJ's Rib Shack.

He shed his coat and hat in the hostess area and walked into the restaurant, with its family-style benches and booths filled with customers, pictures of sepia-toned cowboys and a visual history of Thunder Canyon revealed in a mural painting.

It wasn't two seconds before Ethan came over to him.

"So I hear you've already gotten busy here in town," his older brother said.

Jackson was tall, but Ethan had a couple of inches on him, and he was dressed for the field in boots and jeans since he'd returned from the Bakken Shale today.

It would seem that Big Bro was talking to Jackson about work, yet that wasn't *quite* the case.

Ignoring Ethan's jibe, Jackson headed for a private back dining room where special events were often held, including tonight's family gathering that DJ had called, though no one knew the reason yet.

Ethan followed. "Weren't you the one who said that you'd probably be in Thunder Canyon only long enough to work on this project and then you'd be going back to Midland?"

"That's what I said."

"Well, it sure looks as if you're settling into this place fine enough to me. You're dating a local girl."

Jackson sat at a dining bench. The aroma of DJ's famous rib sauce was already making his stomach grumble.

"It's just a date," he said lightly. "And Laila Cates is fully aware that it's not going to turn into anything more. And just so you know, my social activities won't affect my work here."

Ethan sat across from him. "If you had the kind of track record that didn't include a string of heartbreaks for your dates, I *wouldn't* be worried. From what I know, Laila Cates is the town sweetheart. You mess with her, you mess with every man who's had his eye on her. Traub Oil Montana doesn't need that kind of PR. It's your job to see that this town wants to work with us."

It was obvious that Jackson still had a lot of work to do when it came to earning his family's trust, but he was going to accomplish it. His real dad would've wanted that. Even Pete, his stepfather, would be proud of that sort of determination, and Lord knows that after what Jackson and the rest of his brothers had put

Pete through, the man deserved some consideration.

Good thing that the rest of the Traub kids were coming around to seeing that these days, too, after Pete's heart attack and recovery.

"I don't aim to make trouble," Jackson said, meeting his brother's dark gaze.

Ethan seemed to realize that Jackson meant it—at least for the moment—so he let it go.

That didn't sit right with Jackson, though. He wanted his brother—all his siblings—to know that he was going to come through for them, that he wouldn't screw up again.

He wanted them to have some faith in him.

More of his relatives arrived—Dillon, Corey, their cousins DJ and Dax. A waitress took their orders, then left to place them while everyone made small talk, chatting about their work and lives as well as the latest gossip about ex-town councilman Arthur Swinton and his heart attack and death in jail. He'd been incarcerated for embezzling funds from Thunder Canyon, and his mere name left a sour note in the room.

Drinks were served. Jackson had ordered a soda, showing his brothers that he wasn't such a wild man that he needed a drink in hand at all times. The champagne at Corey's wedding had done enough damage.

Whether or not his siblings noticed the gesture, they ate in peace when the food came.

That was, until DJ brought up some unsettling news.

"Get your fill while you can," he said. He was a quiet man most of the time. Didn't dress flashy, preferring flannel shirts and jeans to a cowboy hat, boasting the same dark eyes and brown hair that seemed to be the hallmark of the Traub family.

Ethan said, "What do you mean?"

DJ put down his fork, then wiped his mouth with a napkin. "I mean that LipSmackin' Ribs is making a play for all the business in town."

And that was obviously the reason he'd brought them together tonight.

A chorus of support for DJ filled the room. Everyone knew that his ribs had a stronghold in Thunder Canyon, as well as other joints sprinkled throughout the country. An upstart rib outfit in the new part of town didn't have anything on DJ's.

Jackson was still taking in the announcement. Strange, but when he'd met Woody Paulson, the manager of LipSmackin' Ribs, a time or two at the Hitching Post bar, the man had never let on that there was an underhanded takeover afoot. He knew that Jackson was a Traub, too.

Had Woody been laughing to himself the whole time, thinking about how he was working over the family right under Jackson's nose?

DJ tried to seem as if he wasn't too worried, but something about his gaze belied that. "LipSmackin' somehow got in tight with the Hitching Post, and they're providing the ribs for them now."

Jackson just shook his head. DJ was decent. Real decent. Never one to screw over a competitor. And Jackson felt protective of that sort of nobility in his cousin.

In his family.

"Let me get this straight," Dax, DJ's brother, said. He was the true rebel of the group and had always reminded Jackson of James Dean in a brooding way. "A tavern that's been in Thunder Canyon for generations has turned its back on one of its own in favor of a bunch of strangers?"

Jackson knew that by *strangers,* Dax wasn't including the Texas Traubs, who had strong family ties to Thunder Canyon. And he could tell that Dax's blood was boiling for the sake of his brother, too.

"This is what they're telling me," DJ said. "I had an exclusive contract with the Hitching Post, but *had* is the operative word." He carefully set down his napkin now. "I'm not going to lie to you all. This is hitting the Thunder Canyon branch of the Rib Shack hard, and it hurts the bottom line of my entire business."

Jackson could see how this affected DJ personally as well. His cousin's skin was a shade of red, as if he was angry, maybe even embarrassed at being treated so shabbily by a neighbor.

And if their neighbors were treating DJ like this, then that left the Traubs to back each other up.

Jackson's jaw had gone just as tight as Dax's appeared to be.

"I can't believe the Hitching Post did this," Dax said.

Dillon, the levelheaded doctor, stepped in. "Maybe there's a good explanation."

"Sure," DJ said. "LipSmackin' Ribs undercut me on cost in a way that the Hitching Post couldn't say no to—not in these economic times. I can't really blame them for accepting the offer, either. It's just good business."

Corey interrupted. "And bad loyalty."

DJ shrugged. "Either way, LipSmackin' Ribs can't possibly be making a profit, from what I can gather. There's just no way."

"Then why the hell are they doing this?" Dax asked.

No one at the table knew.

But all Jackson could gather was that his cousin was hurting, and that was an affront to *him*.

It was something worth fixing.

When he left that night, he didn't go straight home. He drove through Old Town, intending to drop by the Hitching Post since Woody Paulson often stopped there around this time for a drink.

The way Jackson had it figured, brokering a better understanding of the situation would be simple: He was acquainted with the manager of LipSmackin' Ribs in a friendly manner. Why not ask him what was going on?

And who better to do this than the community relations guy for Traub Oil Montana?

Jackson felt good about this constructive method of going about it. He was turning over a new leaf—a diplomatic one.

A helpful one.

He tried to mellow the memory of DJ's wounded expression that kept niggling at him as he walked into the Hitching Post, spying Woody at the bar nursing a brew as the silent jukebox sat sentry in the corner.

Jackson approached the man, a fortyish refugee from Vegas. He still carried some of that old-school air about him in his creased brown trousers and a tan long-sleeved silk shirt that had seen better days.

When he saw Jackson, he raised his mug. "Evening, Traub," he said.

Jackson kept on his coat and declined to order a drink when the bartender approached. Then he greeted Woody right back.

The other man went back to his beer, and that struck Jackson as just being wrong. Here the manager was, part of a scheme to undermine DJ, and he didn't seem to mind at all. It even occurred to Jackson that perhaps Woody had only made a habit of grabbing a drink at the Hitching Post because he'd been making LipSmackin' deliveries all this time.

"I heard about your new contract with the Hitching Post," Jackson said in a civil enough manner. "I suppose congratulations are in order."

Woody froze for the briefest second, then muttered a thanks, but didn't meet Jackson's gaze.

That didn't sit well, either. Jackson didn't like weasels. Didn't like dishonesty on any level.

"It's only unfortunate," he said, doing a fine job of keeping himself in check in spite of his rising dander, "that your business has to be at the expense of my family's."

"It's a cutthroat world out there, Traub. You're a professional man. You know how things are."

"Sure, but as far as memory serves, I never did draw blood from anyone. No one in my family has."

Woody surveyed Jackson, his gaze bleary. "Aren't you the honorable bunch."

Drunk. And just this side of ornery.

Had someone had a bad day?

If Woody hadn't sounded so mocking—as if he'd pulled one over on DJ—and if Jackson hadn't been so swayed by his cousin's genuine sense of concern about his business, he might've let Woody's attitude slide.

Woody stood away from the bar and walked off, and Jackson was about to let him go for the time being.

That is, until Woody looked over his shoulder and bellowed, "Tell DJ that he shouldn't be afraid of a little healthy competition. Tell him to just man up, for God's sake."

Everyone in the bar had gone still, turning to Jackson to see if he was going to stand up for DJ.

Still thinking he could settle this constructively, Jackson followed Woody outside to the boardwalk, near the hitching post that had given the tavern its name.

"Listen, here, Woody," he said. "There's no need to—"

"You're just itching for a fight, aren't you?" the man said, slurring even more.

"No, thank you. But—"

The punch came out of nowhere—a slam of numb pain that blasted into Jackson's jaw.

Instinctively, he punched back, connecting with Woody's eye, sending the man to his rear.

Jackson's knuckles throbbed and he shook them out, sighing. Goddamn it. And he wasn't cursing from the emerging pain in his jaw or hand, either.

"Hellfire," Jackson said. If his dad had been around to see this, he'd be shamed, all right. Awfully shamed. "Now why'd you have to make me go and do that, Woody?"

Woody put a hand over his eye, groaning as Jackson left him, knowing that there would be hell to pay, not only with his conscience, but with his family, too.

Chapter 3

"So how does it feel to be the scourge of Thunder Canyon?" asked Jason Traub on the other end of the cell phone line.

Jackson moved the phone to his other ear while grabbing a coffee from the Town Square cart. The late-morning air nipped his skin as he put a tip in the server's jar, nodded at the man's thank-you, then strolled away, working his sore jaw before answering.

"Being a scourge here doesn't feel any different than being one anywhere else," he said to his twin, who'd called him from Texas after hearing about last night's little scuffle with Woody Paulson.

"You're just damn lucky the man didn't go to the cops. That's all Traub Oil Industries would need, Jackson."

"I know." He'd been beating *himself* up about it, and he was willing to take his own punches. He'd already gotten a few verbal ones from Ethan when he'd shown up in the office early this morning as well. When his older brother had inspected Jackson's jaw, not even finding a bruise, he'd said that Jackson could've used some black and blue to remind him of his misstep.

"Needless to say," Jackson told Jason, "last night wasn't my finest moment. But, believe me, it's *not* gonna happen again."

"Isn't that what you said after Corey's wedding?"

Duly chastised, Jackson wandered to the edge of Town Square, to where a wrought-iron bench waited under an autumn-leafed oak. Around him stood Old West storefronts, comfortable and weathered.

Maybe it was the sight of those old buildings that made Jackson say, "I swear, Jason—I'm making a new start here."

"Beginning when?"

"Now." It was a vow, and he'd never meant anything more in his life.

He really had been fortunate that Woody Paulson hadn't made a bigger deal out of last night. Then again, the other man had thrown the first punch, so it wasn't as if he was innocent in all of it.

But that was no excuse.

Jason wished Jackson the best of luck and signed off, back to his own duties in the Midland offices. Back to his own better-brother-than-Jackson life.

After stuffing his phone into his coat pocket, Jackson took a drink of the black, bracing coffee. He peered farther down the street, knowing just what he would find.

Solace of a sort.

The bank where Laila was working right at this moment.

He smiled, picturing her—blond, blue-eyed, beautiful Laila—and the world seemed right for a moment.

Then again, that was how it always was with him. Women made him feel better, that's all there was to it. And Laila wasn't any different than the rest.

On a whim, he accessed his phone again, dialing what he knew to be her cell number. He'd charmed it out of a friend of a friend of hers after neglecting to have asked her outright for it the other night.

What fun would that have been? The chase was always the best part.

Her phone rang, and when she answered with a curious "Hello?" his heart gave a surprising flip.

Then he reminded himself, *No different than the rest,* and went on.

"Morning, sunshine," he said, taking the chance that she would recognize his voice, even though his number wouldn't have been identified on her phone screen.

When she didn't answer right away, he wondered if he'd been wrong about her remembering him. Laila Cates probably had a hundred men ringing her every morning and calling her "Sunshine."

"Jackson?" she finally asked, and he could've sworn that there was a sparkle in her voice.

But, just as his heart was turning another one of those odd flips, her tone cooled again.

"What can I do for you?"

He laughed. Yup—hadn't he pegged Laila for a challenge right off the bat? "I believe we've got a date to plan."

"Oh?"

"Did you think I forgot?"

"I imagined it wasn't high on your list of priorities. It sounds as if you've been busy with other matters around town."

"Ah." He propped one booted foot on the bench, touching his jaw. "So you heard about last night."

"I told you—news travels fast around here."

Shooting another look down the street, to the stately bank, he pictured Laila at her desk, all polish and prettiness in a business suit. His heart gave a tug.

All he wanted was to see her again.

"Did you ever stop to think," he said, "that if I were to be kept busier, I wouldn't get into so much trouble?"

"Sure. And I can suggest a few things for you to do around Thunder Canyon. You can hike, ride ATVs in the mountains, shop at the resort…"

"I didn't mean to imply that I'd like to do any of those things alone."

He thought he heard her shuffling some papers, and his gut tightened at the image of her being businesslike. He had a thing for serious women, because it was a lot of fun to make them less serious.

"Which one of those would *you* prefer doing?" he asked.

"With you?" She paused just long enough to set him up. "None of the above."

"You're sore at me because I didn't call sooner."

"No, I'm not."

"You don't have to say it. A woman like you is probably used to guys falling all over themselves to set up dates and I neglected to follow protocol."

She huffed out an exasperated sigh, and he grinned.

"Know what sounds good to me?" he asked before he pushed her too far. "A picnic. A good old-fashioned afternoon at the lake. I'll get it all together and pick you up at your place tomorrow at noon."

"But—"

"It's a Saturday, Laila. The best date day of the week."

"I was going to say that there's a chance of rain in the forecast."

He glanced up at the wide, fairly clear Montana sky. He wasn't sure that, besides Texas, he would ever get such a fill of gorgeousness anywhere else.

"I'm willing to take a chance on it," he said. "How about you?"

Of course, he wasn't talking about the weather,

exactly, and she seemed to know it, as several seconds meandered by.

For a moment, Jackson actually thought she was going to turn him down, and the mere possibility shot him straight through with a disappointment he'd never felt before.

But that's why he'd chosen Laila Cates—because she wasn't easy. And because…

Hell, because she did something to his libido.

She finally came back on the line. "Okay. Noon."

Excellent. "See you then, Miss Laila."

As Jackson hung up, he smiled. He'd told his brother, Jason, that he was going to be on his best behavior from now on.

But that didn't necessarily include being a good boy with the woman who'd said yes to spending tomorrow with him.…

Silver Stallion Lake sat in a secluded spot in the mountains. Surrounded by pine trees, it was in October limbo—between the time when winter would bring out the ice skaters and when summer filled the water with swimmers.

Laila cast a glance at the overcast sky just before she laid a blue picnic blanket over the ground. As she sat, spreading out her wool skirt over her boots, pine needles crunched beneath her.

"Not to worry," Jackson said, bringing over a thermal bag, plus a tote of more food, from his rented pickup. "The sky's not going to open up anytime soon."

She ran a subtle gaze over him. Brushed-twill jacket, those jeans that hugged long legs, and scuffed boots. He'd taken off his hat, leaving his hair a dark, heart-poking mess that the slight wind played with.

A trill sang through her, but she told herself that, after this afternoon, there would be absolutely no more dates. She was hoping that Cade would hear about this one, and it would serve its purpose, letting him know that she had—without a doubt—no interest in the marriage he'd suggested.

"You really think you're that persuasive?" she asked Jackson as he returned to his truck and brought back a cooler. "Commanding the weather to do whatever you want it to?"

He offered a cat's-gonna-eat-the-canary smile, and she glanced away before her body did something silly, like flushing so red that she would sigh, just to cool it off.

"I can be persuasive enough," he said, sitting down next to her.

Close.

So close that she could smell the scent of pines—and she knew it wasn't from the trees. It was mixed with the musk of man. Of him.

She reached into the food tote, just for something to do, and started to pull out a loaf of French bread that he'd obviously picked up at the market, along with the bottle of Beaujolais wine he was taking out of the cooler.

As he began to uncork it, she finished unloading the tote—the cheeses, the apples—and got out a plastic plate or two, along with a knife for cutting.

"You certainly know how to stock a picnic," she said, motioning to the wine.

"You know what they say. Somewhere in the world, it's Happy Hour."

"Just not in this part."

He sent her an amused glance, his dark eyes alive with that glint that so often sent her belly spinning.

"Why, Laila," he said, "you're rather prim, aren't you?"

She concentrated on opening a packet of Havarti cheese. "Today? Yes."

"Because you think you need to raise your

defenses with me. Well, I guess I understand why that'd be. You don't know me from Adam. Why shouldn't you be on your guard, especially after everything you've heard about me?"

"Is everything I've heard wrong?"

"Probably not."

She sliced the cheese, careful not to look at him, lest her heart start thudding and she began to think something could happen here. Something fun and...

She put an end to those thoughts. "It's just interesting. You're...different from the rest of your family. Your brothers, at least."

"There're a lot of us. Six, altogether. Standing out ain't such a bad thing."

She finally peered up to find that he'd drawn one leg up so he could lean his arm on his knee. He was looking at the mountains, almost as if he was somewhere else.

Intrigued, she paused in her work, just in time to see him shrug, then pick up an apple and a knife, cutting into the fruit.

"My mom has told me a few times that I remind her of my dad," he said. "My real one. Not my stepfather, Pete Wexler."

The way he said it made her think that he'd

loved his real dad a lot. More than he cared to let on to her.

"Did they get divorced?" she asked. "Your mom and your real dad?"

"No, he died when Jason and I were six. Oil rig accident."

"I'm sorry to hear that."

He didn't say anything for a moment, but she noticed that the cuts he was making to that apple were turning it into a ragged thing.

"Two years down the line," he said in a casual voice, "Mom married Pete. Most of us thought it was too soon, and we weren't what you'd call dream children for him." A smile swiped his mouth. "I might have very well been the worst of anyone."

"And that's how you became a rebel." She thought about the pieces of their conversation from the Hitching Post, tying them into the fragments he was giving her now.

"I guess I did test the new man of the house to his limits," Jackson said, "until I figured out that Pete had a high threshold for tolerance, and he was going to take whatever I, or the others, dished out to him. That's when he earned my respect, even if I wasn't always so good at showing it. I still looked to my older brothers as the leaders of the family, but there was something about Pete's outsider status that I appreciated. And, let me tell you, my mom appreciated that *I* appreciated. Believe it or not, I was the first Traub boy to come around to Pete."

And just when Laila thought they might be having an actual revealing conversation, he peeked from under his lowered gaze, and she knew that he'd just been giving her enough to lead her into another hour of this date. Then another.

He really was an expert tease, doling out information like bread crumbs.

"Your turn," he said, as if daring her.

All right then. "My story is that I know when a man has parsed out just the right amount of information to lure in his date."

He seemed caught off guard by being called out like that, but then he put down the knife and apple, taking out wineglasses from the cooler and pouring the light red liquid into them.

"Well played, Miss Laila," he said. "Well played."

He handed her a glass, and they clinked. A tiny spark of happiness bubbled inside her. She liked trying to keep up with a guy like Jackson Traub.

They drank, and the wine slid down her throat. It seemed to go to her head right away, but that couldn't be right.

Could it be that she was already feeling lightheaded, thanks to him?

It wasn't long before he was back to drawing her out again.

"I hear you've got six kids in your family, too," he said.

"Five girls, one boy. My parents kept trying for a son until Brody, the youngest, came along." Actually, it'd been her dad who'd yearned for a son so badly that Mom had agreed to keep going.

Again, Laila thought of Mom sitting alone at the kitchen table, along with all those college catalogues and a wistful expression.

"A house of girls," Jackson said.

"Don't you go near any of them."

He chuckled.

"I'm serious," she said.

"I wouldn't do any such thing."

"Don't you have a reputation to uphold?"

That's when he got serious, too. "I've got one beautiful Cates woman right here. That's enough for me."

She blushed furiously, and she wasn't sure if it was because he seemed to mean the compliment with every beat of his heart or if it was because he'd used the word *beautiful*.

Couldn't he have said *smart?* Or *engaging?* Or…

She stopped right there. She'd never complained about her looks. It was just that she wished he knew that she brought something more to the table.

For some reason, Jackson had brought the conversation to a standstill.

Was it something he'd said, when all he'd been doing was being genuine?

Whatever it was, a shadow had rolled over Laila's gaze, and it wasn't from the clouds above.

She took a slice of cheese, nibbling on it. He tried not to watch her mouth, the sensuality of each movement, the fullness of those lips he was dying to kiss.

Instead, he got things back on track—if he didn't, there would certainly be no kisses at all.

"See, I need to follow my own advice," he said, lightening his tone. "I told you at the Hitching Post that this kind of talk isn't suited for first dates." And he'd meant it, too, at the time—before he'd gotten way too comfortable here with Laila and found himself telling more than he usually would have.

At his comment, the corners of her mouth turned up, as if she was fighting a smile.

Encouraged, he went on. "So how about those… Hey, what sports teams do you all have here in Montana?"

"College and high school ball. Most don't generally talk about professional sports much around here, unless you're in my house on a Sunday during the fall. That's Football Day—a real big deal. I even forgo sleeping in, and I get up by seven in the morning to take a jog to the Stop 'N' Shop market for chips and dip to bring. It's my big contribution to the festivities."

He didn't want to go back to the family talk. It was too personal, and he'd given up as much as was safe.

"Okay," he said. "Since sports talk isn't the conversational subject of choice here in Thunder Canyon… How was work yesterday, honey?"

The mischievous endearment made her quirk her brow. "Just like any other day, darling."

There. Back on track.

"Rumor has it that you're a real mover and shaker at that bank," he said.

"Sometimes I wonder how much moving and shaking I'm doing, to tell you the truth."

She tilted her head. "Listen to me—I sound like I'm not content with my job."

"Aren't you?"

"Yes. For the most part. It's just that…"

He felt another serious moment coming on, but he didn't stop it. This was where it always seemed to end up with Laila. There was much more to her than he'd expected, and she turned him upside down in more than just the lust department.

Jackson tossed a bit of apple into his mouth. Yup, Laila Cates would've made a good woman for settling down with, if that was in his nature. Or hers.

She still hadn't finished her sentence, so he urged her on.

"It's just that what?"

She gave him a look, as if asking if he was truly interested in this.

She must've read in him that he was.

"It's just that I'm frustrated with my boss," she said. "I've got a proposal sitting on his desk—and not the first one, either—but I can guarantee that he hasn't given it the time of day. You know, he was supportive in promoting me to the manager position, but sometimes I think that he doesn't want me to go beyond that. He's got… I guess you could say old-fashioned ideas of where a woman belongs...and that's below a man."

The shadows Jackson had seen in her gaze earlier had come back now—the same ones that had arrived when he'd pointed out that she was beautiful.

Was this the same woman who'd entered a beauty pageant not a week ago and won with flying colors?

But why had she entered if not for a crown?

He recalled her speech. *Y'all have shown tonight that age and life experience are important—that they add to who we are and how others see us.*

Age and life experience.

Laila wanted to be more than just a beauty queen.

Realizing just now how far out of his depth he was—he was the last man on earth she should've been sitting here with, even on just a lone date—Jackson steered the discussion to where he was more comfortable.

"You ought to turn up the heat inside that bank," he said, teasing again, reaching over to the thermal bag to take out the hot food he'd purchased from the market. "You should march right up to that boss of yours, ask him if he's read your proposal and take names while you're kicking butt. Forget the sweet approach."

"You'd know about kicking butt, wouldn't you?" she asked, but there was a smile there.

It drew his gaze to the beauty spot at the tip of her lips.

Play it slow, Jackson, he thought, as his desire revved right up again.

He spooned some Swedish meatballs—comfort food—onto the plates. "Yes, Laila. I'd know about kicking butt, but I only did it with Woody Paulson because he started up something he shouldn't have."

And Jackson hadn't been smart enough to end it in a better way.

"You know what *you* ought to do?" she asked.

"I'm afraid I'm about to hear."

Undeterred, she gestured to him with her wineglass. "You ought to try the sweet approach instead of kicking butt."

"The sweet approach." What did she think he was—a pansy who liked to tiptoe through the tulips?

His Texas-sized ego cringed at the thought.

But it also let him know that Laila was right, even if he didn't have to be *sweet,* for God's sake.

He would just have to…mellow.

He watched as she leaned back her head, enjoying the day, smiling to herself. The gesture made something glow inside him, too.

Maybe one date wouldn't be enough with her. He had the feeling that he could use more of Laila Cates during his temporary stay here in Thunder Canyon. He needed her kind of balance if he was going to keep his temper as well as his promise to his family.

But could he do that without having this become an actual relationship?

They dug into the meatballs, mashed potatoes and broccoli with Hollandaise sauce that he'd laid out, small-talking about nothing much more than Thunder Canyon. She told him about the gold rush a few years ago, the rise of the resort, the struggles the town had endured.

All the while, he couldn't help but watch her more, wanting her.

Determined that he would have that kiss by the end of the date.

While they cleaned up, stowing the bags and cooler in the tarp-covered back of the pickup, he glanced at the sky once more.

Still cloudy.

But when had clouds ever kept him from anything?

"What do you say we take a walk?" he asked. "Work off some of this food?"

Laila slid a hand to the back of her neck, holding up her blond fall of wavy hair. She flushed, no doubt from the Beaujolais.

"Working off some of those brownies you got for dessert might not be a bad idea," she said.

He took that as a yes and walked away from the truck, waiting for her to catch up.

They didn't talk much as they strolled, just taking in the ruffle of water on the lake from a slight wind, the sound of silence up here in the mountains. A deer darted across their path, coming out from behind a boathouse attached to a dock.

Its hooves thudded on the wood, and as the animal ran toward the pines, its footsteps were cushioned by the dirt. Right afterward, a rabbit sprinted behind the spindly-legged creature, as if scrambling to catch up with it.

Laila laughed. "Bambi and Thumper."

He laughed, too, and their gazes fused.

And, damn if her blue eyes weren't just as big and wary as Bambi's.

His gaze rested on her mouth. Those lips— lush and red and set off to perfection by that beauty spot.

Before he knew it, he was bending closer to her, hearing her soft intake of breath, feeling the heat rumbling through him.

But maybe it wasn't him at all, because her lips formed words.

"Thunder."

Another roll of it shook the sky, just before rain started to patter down.

Just before she took his hand and ran toward the boathouse.

They clattered inside, leaving the door open, laughing just as the sky opened up to let loose a spill of rain.

"What were you saying about clear weather?" she asked, her face damp, her hair just the slightest bit wet—enough for him to reach out and touch it, just to tame a rain-kissed wave.

Then he did what he'd been dying to do before: leaned down to press his mouth to hers.

Chapter 4

Laila had been thinking about what his lips would feel like for the last hour, so she wasn't sure if this kiss was really happening...or if it was just a fantasy.

Because fantasies were a lot *like* this: the pressure of his mouth on hers, wet and warm, at first soft but then growing more insistent with every thud of her pulse. The scent of him—masculine, clean, filling her senses until her head swam and her knees went weak.

This was a kiss.

This was more real than real could have ever been for Laila, and it had taken nearly thirty years for her to get here, to a place where she was feeling a need so deep inside that it actually ached.

But why him—the wrong kind of man for her?

Or maybe the very right one.

She grabbed onto the lapels of Jackson's coat, just as he pulled back ever so slightly—just far enough so that she could still feel his breath on her lips.

"Glad we got that out of the way," he whispered.

She could tell that he was smiling while he said it, even though her eyes were still closed, as if she didn't want to come out of the wonderful haze of this desire.

"Glad?" She finally asked, and she sounded like a dolt. But her brain was in too much of a muddle for it to be functioning properly.

All she wanted was for his lips to be back on hers as the rain tapped away on the roof of the boathouse, imitating the rhythm of her heartbeat.

"I never," he said softly, "leave the first kiss until the end of the date. There's too much jumpiness beforehand. Better to get it out of the way so that you can enjoy that second kiss—the one that comes when a man drops off a woman at her doorstep."

"Just before she invites him inside?" She didn't want to ask how many women had done just that to Jackson Traub. Didn't want to know anything but that he was going to keep on going right here, right now with *her*.

He laughed, and it rumbled through his chest. She could feel the vibration in her fingers, where she was still holding on to his coat.

And that was his only answer.

Then...

Then it wasn't Jackson who continued the kiss.

It was Laila who stood on her tiptoes, putting her hand on the back of his head, winding her fingers through his thick hair and bringing him down to her lips again.

She thought she heard him make a sound—almost a groan—and he wrapped his arms around her, crushing her mouth against his as she lost her balance and stumbled backward until she was against the wall. Something fell from a hook next to them, but she didn't bother to see what it was, although it felt like a length of canvas had come to rest against her leg.

No, she was too lost in him, responding like a wild woman, a perfect match for the notorious Jackson Traub as he brought her against his hard body. His belt buckle dug into her belly when he lifted her and, from the feel of what was beneath that buckle, she realized just how excited he was.

He entered her with his tongue, exploring, making her breathing come so fast that it burned in her lungs. Every inch of her skin was on fire for him and, as they came up for oxygen, she just had time to realize that she was a little bit afraid of what he was doing to her.

Afraid of how close she was to losing *all* control with him.

Sanity was just within her reach, and as he ran his lips over her neck, she had enough time to tell herself to put a halt to this before it was too late.

She had never been "that kind of girl"…

…But when he found the erogenous zone behind her ear with his mouth, she sure wanted to be.

Just a little bit more, she thought to herself while she turned to liquid. *Just a few more minutes....*

But her common sense dissipated in the steam of her craving for him, the chugging of her pulse.

She tugged his shirt out of his jeans, slipping her hands to his waist.

Warm. So warm. And hard with muscle, too.

Her thumbs whisked over the lines of his stomach, and he leaned his forehead against hers.

"What're you asking for, Laila?"

He was warning her, but she didn't care. She just went on and on, smoothing her palms upward, over his ribs, then to his muscle-corded back.

She probably should have heeded his caution, because it was as if she had switched on something inside him.

With another groan, he insinuated his hands under Laila's sweater, mapping her waist with his fingers, with tickling strokes that made her bite her bottom lip. And when he cupped her breasts, she arched away from the wall, urging him on.

He didn't hesitate, unfastening her bra as if he was an expert in hooks and lace. While using his thumbs to circle her nipples, he whispered roughly into her ear.

"Is this what you want?"

She could barely say yes, but she heard the whispering echo of that particular answer inside her, and it came out of her mouth like a gasp. He heard *that,* because he lifted her higher, so that her legs were around his hips now, her sweater bunched so that she could feel the cool air on her skin, her breasts.

When he lowered his head to her, the heat of his mouth took over.

He laved one breast while palming the other. A kiss, a suck, a nip, every motion stabbing her with heat until she felt as if she was being punctured by a feeling so strong, so good that she wanted more lovely pain, more adrenalized hurt.

The ache came to settle between her legs, beating, pulsing, as he took more of her breast into his mouth.

And, still, she wanted him to go on.

He lifted his mouth from her, panting.

Like a wanton thing, she grasped her skirt, pulling on it, inching it up. Asking him without any words.

He laughed softly, understanding what she needed.

He let her slide down the wall a bit, just until she was standing again, held up only by one of his hands while he eased the other under her skirt, between her legs.

With a touch, she nearly exploded.

She gasped as he pressed his fingers against her, then whispered to her again.

"Laila…"

He sounded just as far gone as she was, and that gave her another jolt. A stimulated one.

His passion was the most powerful aphrodisiac of all—better than succeeding in her job. Better than winning the affections of any other man.

Jackson was all that existed for Laila right now.

But then it ended just as quickly as it had begun.

With a long exhalation, Jackson removed his hand, pulling down her skirt without a word, making sure her bra and her sweater were in place.

Confused, Laila stayed against the wall, still pounding with lust.

Had she done something wrong?

He had to have noticed the question in her expression, because he leaned forward, bracing his hand against the wall just over her shoulder.

"The rain stopped," he said.

"What does that mean?" she asked, and she hated that her voice sounded shaky.

Had he merely wanted to prove a point to her?

Dammit, how dumb was she? Falling into the trap set by this well-known scoundrel? He'd probably just wanted to get a piece of the town golden girl.

And he'd sure done it.

"Well, Laila," he said, backing away, tucking his shirt into his jeans. "The rain stopped, and it's a good time to go back outside."

What?

"Jerk," she said, pushing past him toward the boathouse door.

"Laila," he said, sounding truly sorry. "Wait…"

"Stuff it."

"Hey." Then his tone changed back to a scalawag's tease, just as it always did whenever things got a little too serious with him. "I don't want you to think I'm easy, is all."

Now she wasn't just confused, she was mortified as she exited the boathouse, rushing onto the dock, back toward the place where he had parked the truck.

She barely noticed the wet ground, the rainfresh air and its added chill that slapped her cheeks. She was still too heated-up, too…

Turned on.

Damn him, she thought, walking ever faster, as if she could outpace him…

…as well as what had emerged inside her during their time in that boathouse.

As Jackson followed the path that Laila was blazing back to the pickup, he gave her all the room she needed.

Things had gotten *way* out of hand back

there. He hadn't meant to do much more than kiss her, but...

Well, then the woman he had thought was so prim and proper had just up and disappeared, bringing out a Laila who wasn't an ice princess as much as a firebrand.

But what was even more shocking to Jackson was what *she* had brought out in *him*—a protective side, of all things.

A gentleman who hadn't wanted to take advantage of her?

He was still trying to figure that out. With any other woman, he would have taken full grasp of the situation, but there was just something about Laila that made him want to slow everything down.

To savor every moment he would have with her before he left town.

And thank God he would be leaving, because he didn't know how long this side of him would last.

In the near distance, he saw Laila quickly approaching his pickup truck only to come to a full stop, shaking her head, putting her hands on her hips.

She must have just realized that the only ride home she had was with him.

Thinking they could both use a few extra

minutes to cool off, Jackson took his time getting to the truck. Chances were that he came off as being just as arrogant and teasing as usual, but that wasn't the case this time.

He didn't dare poke fun at the situation, so he went straight to the passenger's door and opened it for her, then walked over to his side.

Without a word, they settled into their seats. From the way she was staring straight ahead through the rain-dotted windshield, he had no doubt that he should be glad that he was out of her line of vision. She could've probably cut him in two with just a look right now.

He started the engine, then activated the windshield wipers. They whined across the glass, filling the fraught silence.

Dammit, he couldn't stand this anymore.

"Believe it or not," he said, "you're probably going to thank me later for calling a halt to things."

He should have phrased it differently.

"I *doubt* I'll be thanking you for putting the ultimate whammy on me, Jackson."

"I wasn't putting a whammy on you."

He wanted to tell her that he had gotten just as carried away as she had, but she had already crossed her arms over her chest and, in Woman

Language, that meant she wasn't open to a damn word he might have to say from there on out.

Still, as Jackson drove away from their picnic spot, he didn't let this setback faze him.

To get her this riled up…it meant she actually liked him, right? Laila Cates definitely wasn't one of those women who accepted a date with a man just because she had a carnal itch to scratch. She also wasn't the kind who had dollar signs in her eyes and wanted to get a piece of the action from someone like an oil man with money to burn.

She was genuine.

And he actually liked that about her.

It was a real quiet ride home as all those notions swirled around in Jackson's head; the silence was made even more obvious as the shroud of evening fell around them.

By the time he pulled up to her Old Town apartment building—a quaint redbrick structure with window boxes and garden paths—she had obviously had enough time to stew. And from the way she was clutching the handle of the door, he could tell that she was ready to explode out of the cab the second he pulled into a parking space.

When he parked and cut the engine it didn't

take her but a second to bust out of the truck door, slam it, then make a beeline for her apartment.

Suddenly, Jackson realized how empty the cab felt without her in it.

Rashly, he got out and followed her down the flower-lined path. He got to her door just in time for her to shut it in his face.

All right. Just a little obstacle.

"Laila," he said through the wood. He would take the chance that she might be right on the other side, just waiting for him to leave.

Hell, he could almost feel her there, and he leaned against the doorframe, as if that may bring him closer to her. "You might think that this is the end of it, but it's not."

Next door, a light went on, filtering through the window and onto the damp sidewalk.

Neighbors. Nosy ones at that.

"I aim to change your mind about today, Laila," he said softly. "You're gonna see sure enough that I meant no disrespect to you. That…"

What else could he say?

That I'm smitten with you…?

As if she would believe that. He hardly even believed it himself, knowing it would just be something temporary.

But those were hardly sentiments with which to woo a lady.

He eased nearer to the door, lowering his voice. "If you're there on the other side, listening, hear this—I'm going to win you over before I leave town, Laila. You can bet on that."

Thinking no more was necessary, Jackson sauntered back to his truck, nodding to Laila's elderly neighbor, who was watching through her window.

She pulled back from sight just as Jackson got to his truck, hoping that Laila *had* heard him.

And that she had taken his promise to heart.

Laila had certainly heard every word, and when she went to bed that night, it was with the certainty that she wouldn't be getting much sleep.

She didn't, because she couldn't stop thinking about why Jackson had put on the brakes and, minutes later, told her that he was going to win her over....

Worse yet, when she woke up near the crack of dawn the next morning, it wasn't because her mind was still racing with all the contrary thoughts Jackson had put there. It was because her body was being run through with restless, electric sensations—physical memories of what Jackson had done to her yesterday.

Throwing off her covers, she went to wash up, put on some sweats and read the Sunday morning paper, which she found on her stoop wrapped in plastic, protected from more rain during the night.

"Good morning, Laila," said a voice from the stoop next door.

Laila looked up to find Mrs. Haverly in her quilted yellow housecoat, her gray hair tousled.

"Morning," Laila said.

"Had a bit of excitement last night?"

Oh, man. Her neighbor had apparently been watching the big drama.

"Just a date," Laila said. "That's about it."

"He's cute. I remember back when I could've had a stud like him come courting."

Laila merely laughed, even though Mrs. Haverly had just offered way too much information. Then she held up her paper and wished Mrs. Haverly a good day.

As she closed the door behind her, she thought that it was good to have neighbors— they kept watch when you were gone; they could be like an extended family.

But, darn, they could put their noses where they didn't belong.

The central heating kicked on, and Laila plopped onto her beige faux-leather couch.

It matched the rest of the room, which she'd decorated with the restrained hand of someone who liked paintings by Renoir, fake green plants and a sleek home-theater unit.

Next to her, on an end table, was the only thing in life that Laila needed to take care of—Lord Vader, whose goldfish colors weren't exactly reminiscent of a dark villain. But when Laila had purchased a tiny Death Star model to go inside the fishbowl, she couldn't resist the name.

She laid her head on the back of the couch, watching Vader swim around.

"What do *you* think?" she asked. Of course, her fish wouldn't answer, but talking to her pet was better than talking to herself. "Should I give Jackson Traub a chance to explain himself?"

Vader went on swimming, hardly giving a hoot.

"I know—why should I be fretting about this when he's going to be gone soon enough, anyway? And why should I even care about *that* when I'm not even looking for someone to keep on dating?"

Laila sighed because she already had her answer, even without talking to Vader. She *enjoyed* being with Jackson. More than enjoyed, actually, based on how she had reacted to him in the boathouse.

Vader disappeared behind the Death Star, and Laila raised her head from the couch, thinking that this flagrant lack of concern from her pet was not a good sign. Or maybe she was just listening to her better instincts now.

Would she do well to cut her losses with Jackson immediately, avoiding any more entanglements?

Yeah, that was probably the safest way to go about this. She'd had her one date with the cowboy and wasn't beholden to him to go on another.

Ignoring the knot that had formed in her stomach, she finished reading the paper. After that, when she was just leaving her apartment to take her usual jog to the market for Football Day bean dip and chips, she told herself that she was already feeling better without Jackson. It could even be that Cade would soon hear about her date with the Texan, since Mrs. Haverly was known to be a gossip, and Laila's purpose for going out with Jackson in the first place would have come to fruition.

She put on a pair of sneakers, grabbed a tote bag, then went outside to brave the cloudy morning. She never listened to music while she jogged on the way to the market then walked back—the distraction seemed sacrilegious here in Thunder Canyon, where there was so much to appreciate: the song of birds, the stillness of the air, the trees all around her.

It was a quick trip to the market, and as she started her walk back to her apartment, she hardly even minded that she looked a tad disheveled in her sweats with her hair in a messy ponytail and wearing very little makeup.

At least, she didn't mind until she walked out of the parking lot and onto the road, where, after a few minutes, she heard the purr of an engine behind her.

Glancing over her shoulder, she recognized the blue pickup immediately.

Her heart just about rammed out of her chest. Jackson?

She resisted the temptation to sprint. Good heavens, she had almost forgotten how she had told him about her normal Football Day morning run yesterday during their picnic.

But she still remembered what he had said just before he had left her alone last night.

I'm going to win you over before I leave town, Laila. You can bet on that.

As her pulse jigged, his truck pulled up alongside her, but she kept from looking over at him.

Her body hummed, remembering.

Wanting.

"Need a ride?" he asked through the open passenger-side window. He was as friendly as could be, as if there had never been any hard feelings between them.

"I'm fine." She started to walk faster, but realized it wouldn't do any good.

Then she became ultra-aware that she was in sweats—and that she hardly looked like a beauty queen.

But wasn't that a good thing? Maybe she would scare him off.

As usual, he was persistent. "Are you sure you don't need a lift? It's not out of my way."

Laila couldn't stand another half hour of him dogging her.

She halted, hands on her hips, and he stopped the truck. Behind him, the road was empty.

"Jackson, what're you doing?"

He seemed bewildered at so simple a question. "I'm offering you a ride."

She blew out a breath. "Why are you on this road, first thing in the morning, on my side of town?"

She knew that he was staying in a condo up at the resort. Renting, naturally.

He offered her a maddening, charming grin.

"I know this is your Sunday routine, so I took the chance that I might catch you here."

"Were you waiting in the market parking lot for me?"

"Yeah, but I stayed occupied. Brought the paper with me." Another grin, telling her that he was aware that he had skirted her main point.

She would have liked to smack that grin right off his face if it wasn't so...

Endearing?

Great.

Then his grin mellowed. "I just want to talk to you, Laila, clear the air. I don't like the way we left things last night."

A flutter of excitement in her belly made her put a hand there, yet she took it away before he could notice.

But she might have been too late on that, based on the way his gaze had followed her gesture.

In spite of what her body was doing to her, she was damn sure going to keep to what she had vowed this morning—that she wouldn't have anything more to do with trouble.

"We don't suit each other, Jackson," she said, hoping *that* would put him off once and for all. "And I'm sorry you had to hang around the market all morning to hear that."

He seemed to fight a smile. Was he remembering just how well they suited in the boathouse?

"What I mean," she said, "is that you're a playboy. Your lifestyle doesn't mesh with mine in general."

"This, from a woman who's had suitors since she first learned to bat her lashes."

She was just about to offer her next retort when he delivered the capper.

"Aren't *you* something of a playgirl?"

His reasoning tied up her tongue.

Was she just that—a playgirl? She had never thought of herself that way before, but if she was applying a certain definition of the term to *him,* why wasn't it good enough for *her,* too?

She was a playgirl who had never wanted to settle down, who had broken hearts without meaning to.

And she was probably just like Jackson.

"We really are two of a kind," he said, his arm curved over the steering wheel, careless, casual.

That was when yet another truth hit her, right along with the first one. She realized that Jackson was looking at her just as he always did—with appreciation. This entire time, he hadn't even seemed to notice that she wasn't all dolled up.

Whether she liked it or not, that scored a few points with her.

"Laila," Jackson said, and the sound of her name coming from him was what finally did her in. He had a way of saying it that gave her pleasant shivers.

"Give me another chance," he said.

She wanted to tell him to get lost, but she was sure that her expression said something else entirely.

Jackson smiled, encouraged. "One more chance. That's all I'm asking for. Tomorrow night, after you get off work. I'd like to take you to the Gallatin Room up at the resort."

He was pulling out all the stops, offering to bring her to the fanciest restaurant in Thunder Canyon. Still stubborn as hell, though, she was going to make him work even harder than that.

"I don't know," she said.

"Come on, Laila."

The way he said her name…

Dang it, she couldn't resist. Why not just *one* more date?

"Okay," she said.

"Great." He sat back in his seat. "I'll pick you up at your place. Seven o'clock?"

"Seven's fine." Boy, how did she manage to sound as if he wasn't rocking her world?

Now that they had everything straight, he was back to the first order of business. "Are you sure you don't want that ride?"

"No, thank you." She wasn't about to give him a close-up view of Workout Laila Cates, no matter how much he seemed not to notice her dishabille. "I'll just see you tomorrow."

"Good enough." He put the truck in gear. "And Laila?"

She lifted an eyebrow in query.

He jerked his chin at her. "I like how you wear that saucy ponytail."

With that, he drove away, leaving her to think that even though she had refused his ride today, she was bound to get a wild one tomorrow night.

Chapter 5

"The Gallatin Room," said Laila's younger sister, Jasmine, with a sigh as she, Laila and the other three Cates girls gathered in the kitchen at the family ranch just before the first football game of the day. "He's taking you to the *Gallatin Room*."

Holding back a dizzy grin, Laila nodded while putting her tortilla chips into a plastic bowl. The reality of her next date with Jackson had set in, making her a little nervous now.

Nervous, but almost embarrassingly excited.

Her youngest sister, Abby, said, "Fancy times, Laila."

She sent a smile to Abby, who, in her early

twenties, had always grown up in the shadows of all the Cates sisters. But with her long brown hair and big brown eyes, she had just as much going for her as the rest of her family.

Not that she seemed to know it, though.

Laila wished she could tell Abby as much while her youngest sister put together a salad, and Jasmine arranged other snacks on the kitchen table. Annabel and Jordyn helped her.

Jasmine said, "Jackson Traub's a real looker. Does he have any brothers just like him?"

Jordyn and Annabel laughed at Jazzy's usual enthusiasm for the opposite sex.

"He's got a twin in Texas," Laila said. "But I can't speak for his status."

Her sister flipped her long blond ponytail off her shoulder. "Oh? When's *he* coming to Montana?"

"Don't know."

Jordyn interrupted, still terribly interested in Laila's business. "So is Jackson as crazy as everyone is saying he is?"

Crazier, Laila thought.

"He's got his moments," she said.

As Laila brought her snack bowls to the table, Annabel snagged a tortilla chip.

"He punched out Woody Paulson," she said. "He sounds kind of dangerous."

"Dangerous?" Laila laughed. Not for an instant had she ever felt in danger being around Jackson. In fact, he made her feel…

She wanted to say "right at home," but was that really the case? Because oftentimes, she wasn't sure that the propulsion of the blood through her veins was very comfortable at all, even if she liked it.

She felt herself blushing and hoped none of her sisters noticed. "He's not that bad. Jackson's just…a good-time guy."

"Mr. Right Now," Jazzy added.

"Not quite." Laila leaned against the table. "He's more like Mr. Defies Definition."

"That's just a short-term thing," Jordyn added, stealing a chip before Annabel could snag another one from the bowl. "Laila, once you get to know him better, he could be a catch, and you'd be a fool to discount him this early on."

"Yeah," Annabel said, smacking away Jordyn's hand from the chip bowl. "Why are you just going on one more date with him and putting the kibosh on any more than that? You should give him more of a chance."

Behind the kitchen counter, where Abby was gathering silverware, Laila thought she heard a chuff, as if her youngest sister was thinking that Laila didn't give many men a chance.

Little did Abby know that Jackson had gotten *quite* the opportunity just yesterday at the lake.

Laila's skin burned every time she thought about him pressed against her, his body hard and ready...

She cleared her throat, thinking that it was almost time for the blessed game kickoff, and she would be able to escape this sisterly grilling and get to the family room.

"Jackson," she said, attempting to end the topic, "isn't going to be around Thunder Canyon long enough for there to be much of any chance, girls."

"Okay, then," Annabel said. "So he'll be out of here soon. But, in the meantime, if Jackson's a good-looking guy with plenty of money and, as usual, you're not seeking a permanent commitment, why limit yourself?"

Jordyn wagged her finger in Laila's direction kiddingly. "That's all you do is limit yourself, Laila. Just ask poor Cade Pritchett."

Abby dropped a piece of silverware in the kitchen, and everyone jumped.

"Sorry," Abby said.

Jazzy didn't pay any attention to that. "Laila, if you ask me, you're just plain crazy. Jackson Traub's a hunk. I'd totally get as much out of him as *I* could."

Abby said from the kitchen, "No one is good enough for perfect Laila."

It sounded as if she was ribbing Laila just as lightly as her other sisters were, but there was a slight prickle to Abby's tone. Laila had always had the feeling that her youngest sister thought she didn't deserve all this attention from guys.

She only wished she knew what was going on with Abby today. She wasn't usually like this, except when it came to talking about men.

Just as Laila was about to ask, the sliding glass porch door opened, and Dad ducked his salt-and-pepper haired head inside.

"Ready for the beef?" he asked.

Jazzy laughed, no doubt thinking about the meat market they had just been talking about.

Dad stepped inside, and the aroma of barbecue slipped in, too, right along with Laila's twenty-year-old brother, Brody, who was carrying a plate of grilled steak strips for soft tacos.

Laila couldn't help but poke fun at Dad. "Looks like it's time for your team to lose, Pop."

He glanced pointedly at the Montana State Bobcats sweatshirt she was wearing with her jeans. "Little girl, your team doesn't even have any skin in today's NFL game. You rooting for the Chiefs?"

"If you're rooting for the Broncos…then yup."

It had always been this way—Laila getting Dad's and Brody's goats by cheering for the opposite football team on game day. Dad had gone to college in Colorado, taking up the fever for the state's professional team, too, and he'd passed along his Bronco enthusiasm to his only son. Laila had no allegiances, though—even if, on occasion, she would give in and root for the Broncos, just to make the men in the family happy.

Her sisters, who cared more about the food and the company on their Sundays together than the games themselves, had already lost interest and were beginning to load up their plates.

But Brody was a different story. He pointed at Laila in challenge. "You gonna put your money where your mouth is? How much you have?"

"The usual twenty," Laila said. "And I'll use my winnings wisely after the Broncos lose."

Mom entered the room at that point and, even though Evelyn Cates came off as being at least ten years younger than her fifty-one years, it was like looking into a mirror of the future for Laila. She only hoped that there wouldn't be a slightly regretful shade of blue in her own eyes.

"I hear you throwing down the gauntlets in here," Mom said.

Without comment, Abby passed her on the way out of the room, and Mom shot an "Is she okay?" look to Laila.

She merely shook her head, unable to explain. Whatever the case was, though, soon she was going to have a good sit-down with Abby, getting to the bottom of whatever was bugging her sister.

"Is all forgiven?" Jackson asked DJ that afternoon in the Rock Creek Diner, a newer place in Old Town where Jackson had requested they touch base, just so he could make sure he hadn't caused his cousin more grief after the Woody Paulson incident.

DJ, dressed in a flannel shirt and jeans, stretched an arm over the back of a red-upholstered booth near the front of the establishment. Nearby, at the lunch counter, a few ranch hands were watching the Chiefs/Broncos game, drinking beer and eating burgers.

"Don't worry about a thing, Jackson," DJ said. "I might've laid into Woody the way you did. I just wasn't there to do it."

"Thanks for saying so."

"Hey, you didn't make matters any worse with LipSmackin' Ribs than they already were."

A waitress in braids delivered their food—a Reuben for DJ and a big bowl of chili plus thick sourdough bread for Jackson. They thanked her, and for the first time in Jackson's life, he didn't watch a waitress walk away.

It was just that he didn't have the urge, and that gave him pause.

Did it have anything to do with Laila?

His pulse did a few jumping jacks, and he thought it better to stop thinking about her, even though it had been a near impossibility since seeing her this morning and managing to wheedle another date out of her.

He must have been wearing a goofy kind of smile, because DJ said, "What's got you so giddy?"

Jackson just shrugged, trying not to offer any more of a tell on his face.

His cousin chuckled. "Heck, I already know about your date with Laila Cates. No reason to explain."

Jackson had just been about to dig into his chili, but his spoon remained poised above the bowl.

Was it that obvious?

He didn't like being so transparent. It made

him feel stripped bare for a second, and he scrambled to cover up.

"What makes you think I'm getting giddy about Laila Cates?" he asked.

At the lunch counter, he thought he sensed a shifting, so he decided to keep his voice down.

"Whoa," DJ said, hands up. "Didn't mean to ruffle your feathers."

"I'm not ruffled."

Again, he thought he heard something at the lunch counter. A laugh?

When he glanced over, he saw a couple of cowboys looking at each other, as if they knew what it meant to be ruffled by Laila Cates. Maybe they had even had their hearts broken by her. Who knew?

Jackson's bachelor pride burned. Worse yet, he even felt as if something was slipping inside him—out and away.

Before he could think twice, he said, "It's not as if I'm shedding my ways for anyone."

Not even Laila?

The stray thought bashed into him, but it had no place in his head.

"I see," DJ said, even though it appeared as though he didn't—not with that grin he had going as he bit into his sandwich.

"Laila's about the most beautiful woman

I've ever seen, and who could resist that? But when I leave Thunder Canyon, I'll leave. No looking back."

Out of his peripheral vision, he saw one of the ranch hands at the counter glance over his shoulder, and when Jackson looked over, he recognized him as a guy who'd been at the Hitching Post the other night—the mustached, silver-buckled cowboy who'd seemed more interested than anyone else when Jackson had sat down at Laila's table.

Now the man's gaze seemed flinty, as if there was a trace of hard jealousy there, and instead of feeling like the cock of the walk, Jackson just felt as if he had done a wrong to Laila by being so flippant about her.

Before he could say something else to DJ—something that could explain the careless remark he had made—the door to the diner dinged open, and a man and a woman walked through.

At first, the sight of the female's blond hair and blue eyes threw Jackson for what was definitely a giddy loop. But it was only because he was still thinking of Laila, as if she owned some part of him already.

Then he realized that *this* woman wasn't Laila at all, and the brown-haired, green-eyed man in jeans and cowboy boots with her wasn't just any old guy.

It was Zane Gunther, the country music star.

Everyone in the diner turned in their seats to see him, not only because of his fame, but because he had become a true part of Thunder Canyon lately, after going through a passel of trouble. A young girl had died after one of his concerts, and her parents had brought a civil suit against Zane and his promoter.

He was holding the blond woman's hand, and Jackson remembered her name now. Jeannette Williams.

There was something special between them. Something that gave a tweak in Jackson's chest.

The hostess went over to the couple. Other people in the diner did the same, including DJ, who shook their hands.

Putting down his napkin, Jackson followed, thinking the singer could use all the support he could get right now, with his trial coming up in December.

"So good to see the two of you," said the hostess, a matronly woman with fluffy brown hair.

Zane smiled. "We thought we'd grab a meal before heading down to Austin."

"What's in Austin?" asked an old man who leaned against the back of a booth.

"We've got some preparation and depositions to take care of for the trial," Zane said.

DJ spoke up. "You let us know if you can use any character references or anything."

The group reinforced DJ's comment, and the hostess said, "We're behind you all the way."

Zane and Jeannette seemed touched, and he gripped her hand all the tighter.

"Thank you for that," he said. "You don't know how much it means to hear it."

Just as it seemed the greetings were over, the hostess squealed, then grabbed Jeannette's hand.

"And what's *this?*" she asked.

Now that Jackson looked closely, he could see what the hostess was talking about. On Jeannette's finger, a heart-shaped diamond ring glittered.

As everyone oohed and ahhed, Jackson faded back into the crowd. The sight of an engagement ring made him…itchy.

But the loving looks that Zane and Jeannette were exchanging got to him just as much. It was obvious that with this woman, Zane was going to come through whatever challenges he had to face.

What would it be like to have someone like that by his side, too?

Jackson dismissed the thought. It just felt a little empty to know that some men were built to be with a significant other, and some weren't. There were no doubts where *he* stood.

After Zane and Jeannette told everyone that they were hoping to get married on Valentine's Day, they thanked the crowd again and were ushered to their booth. DJ and Jackson returned to sit at their own table.

"Nice couple," Jackson said, just to make conversation, hoping that DJ wouldn't talk about Laila again.

"Things are going well for them." DJ wrapped his fingers around his soda glass. "Zane's going to come out of that legal mess just fine, and as for Jeannette, her job helping with Frontier Days led to her getting a position as an administrative assistant in the mayor's office. They've had a hard run of it recently, but life has turned around for them. Good things couldn't happen to better people."

Jackson agreed, and that was why he didn't ever expect there to be any "good things" like diamond rings or Valentine's Day marriages in his future.

The next night, Laila had gotten ready for her second date with Jackson *way* too early, and she was fairly bubbling with anxiety as she sat on her sofa—something she had been doing for about a half hour now.

She ran her hands down the dark blue dress she had chosen. It was straight, silky and maybe a little too sexy with the strappy pumps she had paired with it. And her hair… Was it better to leave it up in this French starlet style or take it down?

She glanced over at her fishbowl, where Lord Vader was happily swimming about.

"Am I overdoing it?" she asked her pet. "Is he going to think I care way more about this date than I actually do?"

Her fish could've given a flying fig.

Some confidant.

But watching Lord Vader swim did calm Laila a bit—not enough to still her heart, though. It was just that she kept thinking about the advice her sisters had given her yesterday, how they had encouraged her to keep seeing Jackson, even if there wasn't a future with him.

So why be nervous if this was such a casual, fun fling?

When she saw a flash of headlights through her curtains, she stood up, adrenaline racing.

But she didn't go to the door. Not yet. It would be catastrophic if Jackson thought that she had been just waiting here for him like some old maid who didn't have anything better to do.

He knocked, and she counted to five, grabbed her coat from the sofa, blew a kiss to Lord Vader, then answered.

She opened the door to find Jackson standing there just as long and lean and cocky as usual. But then...

Something happened.

She couldn't explain it, other than that it was a change in the cool air, a shift of feeling and perception.

He looked her up and down, took off his cowboy hat and held it over his chest.

"Laila," he said.

And she couldn't even say his reaction was caused by how gussied up she was. He had worn the same look yesterday morning, when he had caught her walking back to her apartment in her sweats.

It was almost as if she took his breath away just by standing near him....

Normally, she would've handled the situation with aplomb. She was used to compliments, although she appreciated the sentiments that went behind every single one of them.

But this?

This was something else.

She didn't know what to do but say, "I decided against the sweatsuit tonight."

His gaze seemed hazy, and she even thought she saw him swallow with more difficulty than usual.

Without saying anything more, he reached out his free hand.

His gesture seemed to mean much more than just helping her out the door. Taking his hand seemed to signal that she was going someplace new, different.

Impulsively, she nestled her hand in his and, right away, a kick of desire jarred her.

All he had to do was touch her and she got shaky.

Good heavens.

After closing her door, they walked the short distance to his pickup. During the ride up to the resort, he turned on the radio, covering their lack of conversation.

By the time they got there, Laila had composed herself, silently repeating again and again that she had dated *plenty* of good-looking guys before, that she had always been in control of romantic situations and she should have no problem doing that now.

The Gallatin Room, which had a muted

ambiance, featured a spectacular view of the mountains. The maître d' sat them at the best table in the house, in front of the window, candlelight flickering from a frosted-glass sconce.

Laila opened the menu, having no idea what she would order, even though she had been here a couple of times before—neither of which had made her freak out like *this*.

"I don't know if I'm excessively spoiled," Jackson said, pulling her out of her jitters, "but I've been to so many fancy restaurants that I always know what I want straight off."

His voice, low and mellow, went a long way toward smoothing out her anxiety, and she lowered the menu. "This is what you do for Traub Oil? Take people out to nice places?"

"It's what I *did* do at Traub Oil in Texas. As you can imagine, I'm pretty good at courting clients."

Um, yeah. She imagined he had cornered the market on courting a long time ago.

"And what exactly do you do now, here in Montana?" she asked.

"They call it community outreach. See, one of your local boys, Austin Anderson, has got an engineering background, and he's working on more environmentally beneficial ways to extract oil from the Bakken Shale. I'm in charge of educating people about the developments on that front. And I'm here to be a liaison between Traub Oil Montana and the people we leased or bought land from in the Shale."

It was a more mature position than he'd had before, she realized. "How do you like the switch?"

"From party boy to responsible citizen?" He grinned. "It's working so far, as long as I don't meet up with Woody Paulson again."

"And as long as you don't have any more brothers who get married?"

"A point to the lady."

His gaze glittered in the candlelight, and she had to glance back at her menu before she slid down in her chair like wax going hot and slippery under the heat of fire.

She still couldn't make up her mind about the food, but being unable to make decisions wasn't exactly a new thing when she was around Jackson.

"The *coq au vin* is always good," he said.

"Sounds perfect to me." She wasn't exactly sure what it was since the description didn't offer many details, but she trusted him.

She shut her menu, just in time for the waiter to arrive and introduce himself, plus the specials of the night. When the sommelier came, she recommended a Pinot Noir from Oregon to be paired with the *coq au vin,* which Jackson was also having.

Soon, they were breaking artisan bread from a basket, dipping it in olive oil. All the while, Laila couldn't keep her mind straight, since it kept wandering to places it shouldn't stray: places like the boathouse, where she had let him—and herself—go way too far. Like the front seat of his pickup, where she wondered if he was going to try to kiss her again tonight.

Like the bedroom, where, if she wasn't careful, they might end up.

But they wouldn't. God help her, they *couldn't,* because even if he wasn't in Thunder Canyon long term, that didn't mean she would suddenly forget her pride and become someone who slept with anyone.

Still, she couldn't stop thinking of Jackson's fingertips on her skin, stroking over her until the hair raised on her arms and until she went tight in her belly, warm and curdled...

"What's going through that head of yours?" Jackson asked, and it seemed to come out of the blue of her fantasies.

She sat up in her chair, dabbing the napkin over her mouth to buy herself some time. If she said anything right now, she just might stammer.

"Nothing much," she finally managed.

"Aw, don't tell me that, Laila. You're a complex woman."

Slowly, she looked up at him. Complex?

She remembered how he hadn't seemed to care that she had been wearing a sweatsuit yesterday, how he had looked at her as if she was, for all the world, perfect in his eyes.

As if she didn't have to dress in anything but herself for him.

"I'm thinking," she said, turning her gaze to the window and the view, "that this is a really good night, Jackson, and that I'm glad I came."

When she turned to him again, she saw that he had gotten that roguish grin on his face, and she knew that he was just as happy to get away from serious subjects as she was.

"The night's hardly over," he said softly, making her stomach whirl.

Making her wonder, once more, what would come at the end of this date.

Chapter 6

The night was like a stretch of never-ending torture for Jackson as he sat across from Laila in the Gallatin Room, yearning for her with such ferocity that he thought he might be pulled apart long before he drove her home.

He managed to last through the main course, dessert, the slow walk they took through the boutique hall of the resort, then to his truck.

It was yet another quiet ride home, but unlike the last time, on the way back to town from Silver Stallion Lake, the silence was weighted with something other than hard feelings.

He could feel the air just about vibrating between them, humming with possibility, and he knew she was wondering what kind of moves he planned to make.

Part of Jackson wanted to go for it—seduce her as he would seduce any other woman. But, with Laila, he didn't want this anticipation to end. It was too enjoyable, like a fine bourbon you would nurse, reveling in the taste, the warmth slipping down from throat to belly.

When they reached her apartment building, he pulled into a different parking space than he normally used; around the corner, away from the windows, near a maple tree that somewhat blocked them from view.

He allowed the engine to idle, leaving on the radio, which was playing an old Charlie Rich tune. The singer was mulling about what happens behind closed doors, after two people find themselves alone for the night.

Just like now.

Laila hadn't opened her door yet, and Jackson wondered how long he could keep her here, her citrus-breeze scent filling the truck's cab.

She finally glanced at him from under those lush eyelashes, smiling a little. "Thanks for tonight. It was nice."

Lord knew how she did it, but she made his heart buck.

"Nice," he said, repeating her description. "That's all it was?"

"You know what I mean."

She tucked a long blond strand that had escaped from her upswept style behind her ear just as Charlie Rich sang the part about how his woman lets her hair hang down...and how she makes him feel glad that he's a man.

And Jackson felt all man right about now, too, with his heartbeat traveling downward, lower and lower until it pained him.

Take it slow, he reminded himself. *No reason to rush when the buildup is so good.*

Laila gave him another long look, and she must have seen what she was doing to him, because she got a glint in her eyes—the kind of glint *Jackson* was known for. At least, that was what they told him.

It was confident.

Bold.

Jackson's pulse double-timed.

"So," she said, her voice low and throaty. "I guess we've fulfilled our date quota."

"A quota."

"You asked for just one more, and here it was."

He wanted to say that it wasn't enough—that he couldn't even think of being in Thunder Canyon, knowing she was there, too, yet never seeing her again.

"Laila," he said softly, resting his arm on the back of the seat, his hand so close to her shoulder that his fingertips tingled. "There can be a lot more to come."

She swallowed, and he noticed that the windows around them were paling from the bottom up with the beginnings of steam.

Before she could give him a sassy rejoinder, he eased closer to her, subtly yet surely.

He was so near that he could hear her intake of breath as if it was his own.

"We're going to see each other again," he said. "Don't you doubt it."

"You assume quite a bit," she whispered.

He drew even closer, to where he knew she would feel his breath on her mouth.

"I assume enough to know what you're dying for me to do right now."

And he leaned in the rest of the way, fitting his mouth over hers.

In a roaring burst, he was enveloped in passion and heat, her lips parting, responding. Her hands gripping his coat and pulling him closer.

Without thinking, he wrapped her in his arms, dipping her back against the door as she bent her leg, nestling even nearer to him.

A flash of desire split him in two, and he felt as if they were in that boathouse again, with him losing all mental faculties, with him needing her so damn much that it scared the wits out of him.

He pulled back a little from her, looking down at this woman who captivated him and made him want to say things he shouldn't ever say to anyone. He looked at that beauty-queen face, but it wasn't her prettiness that got to him—there was something in her gaze that pulled him in with even more inexplicable force.

It was deep inside her, down in the blue of her eyes. There, he thought he might even be able to see a quality that she had never shown anyone else before, though he couldn't be sure.

The sight of it shook Jackson to the core, causing him to stop altogether.

Too far, he thought. One more step, one more kiss, and he was going to cross a line he might never bc able to go back over.

And what would he do with her then?

What would *she* do with him, once he started to disappoint her with his inability to commit?

Gently, he tweaked her cheek with a finger, then let her go, moving to his side of the truck with a grin that covered his disappointment at having to pull back.

Some men were born to be good for others. He wasn't one of those. Never had been, never would be.

The furrow of Laila's brow made him all the more rankled until she gathered herself, smoothing out her dress and buttoning her coat.

"Well, Jackson," she said, "if I didn't know any better, I'd say that you're a pro at playing hard to get."

She didn't sound angry this time, maybe because she had already known what she was in for with him. And, oddly enough, that made Jackson feel the slightest bit better. If they both knew what to expect from each other, there would be no more disappointment.

"You've got me," he said, holding out his hands, as if in surrender.

"Do I?"

She said it with a bubbled laugh, and if he didn't know any better, he would've thought that there was a pop of frustration beneath it.

For a moment, he got more serious than he had ever intended.

"Yeah, Laila. You've definitely got me."

The air seemed to go still, probably because he meant it—at least in the heat of this moment.

He didn't trust himself to mean it tomorrow...or anywhere down the road.

She opened the door, snapping the tension apart. "Thanks again. I really am glad we went out."

He watched her get out of the truck, then stroll away. Common sense told him to stay put, to leave her be, but then he found himself climbing out of the cab, too, walking toward her door, where he'd just say a last good-night then leave.

She was unlocking her front door when he approached her bottom step, and he remained there, all too certain that he wouldn't be able to stop himself from going inside if she gave him even the slightest indication that this was where she wanted to take the date.

It was as if she knew better than to ask him in, too, and she gave him a little grin.

"Drive home safe," she said, taking her time in closing the door while the light from behind her made her hair golden.

"Just promise me you're going to kick some butt at that bank tomorrow," he said, as if he couldn't stand for the night to end.

She paused, apparently remembering their conversation a couple days ago during their picnic.

Then she shrugged. "I'll kick butt only if *you* refrain from it. How's that for a deal?"

"Sounds reasonable."

She laughed, shut the door all the way, and when the lock clicked into place, it was as if something inside Jackson had been closed, too, just begging to be opened again.

Jackson had gone home and taken a good cold shower. It had done its part in getting his head—and the rest of him—back together, but the next day during work, he found himself at his desk, staring out the window in the direction of Laila's bank.

Of course, he couldn't see it from here, but just knowing that she was merely five minutes away was killing him.

He got through a day of setting up meetings with some of the families that Traub Oil Montana was leasing land from, but he called off work when his brother, Ethan, stuck his head inside the door.

"Got a minute?" he asked.

"Today I have more minutes than I know what to do with," Jackson said, thinking of all the time he would have to fill when he went back to his condo tonight. Every one of those minutes would be punctuated by his longing to see Laila again.

"We've got an impromptu family meeting going on in the conference room," Ethan said.

Without any more information, his sibling disappeared. Jackson got up from his desk, thankful for the interruption until he walked into the conference room to see his brothers, Dillon and Corey, plus Dax, at one end of the long table. His younger sister, Rose, who had been in PR and communications for Traub Oil until she'd begun working in Mayor Bo Clifton's office, was standing just under a mounted TV screen, her arms crossed. Their expressions were stoic enough, but the look on DJ's face was the worst.

Jackson took a seat next to his cousin. "What's going on?"

Corey said, "We're here to hammer out what we're going to do about this brewing rib war once and for all."

DJ said, "After our last meeting, Dillon reminded me that this shady business maneuver from LipSmackin' Ribs wasn't the first—just the most blatant. You all know Zane Gunther's fiancée, Jeannette, used to work at the other joint for a time."

Everyone nodded.

Dillon, who was good friends with Zane, took over. "Jeannette had told me that, before she left her job with LipSmackin' Ribs, she was asked to spy on DJ's Rib Shack."

"I didn't take it seriously at the time," DJ said.

Corey jumped in. "But then their ribs started tasting like DJ's. They must have found *someone* who agreed to spy on the Rib Shack."

Ethan rested a shoulder against the wall, near a window. "In hindsight, now we know that Jeannette's news should've been taken more seriously."

"How seriously are we going to take it now?" Jackson's blood was beginning to simmer again, just as it had the night when he had gone to talk to Woody at the Hitching Post. And seeing DJ with his expression so solemn only made Jackson's temper rise all the more, even though he had promised to control it.

But that felt nearly impossible.

"I'm with Jackson," Dax said, his leather jacket creaking as he leaned forward. Then he addressed the whole family. "I've been telling DJ since our last meeting that LipSmackin' Ribs is going beyond traditional competitive marketplace tactics. And we're here now because I, for one, think that Woody Paulson made this whole thing very personal when he threw a punch at Jackson. I don't know what's going on, but it's not just business."

"Hey, now," Dillon said. "I'm sure that both Woody and Jackson would admit that things just got out of hand between them."

In other words, the fight hadn't been entirely Woody's fault, Jackson thought. Half of him wanted to sink down in his seat at that, anticipating the looks he might get from his family. But the other half?

It wanted to fight, not only for DJ, but for the entire family's honor.

"So what are we going to do about LipS-mackin' Ribs then?" Jackson asked.

No one spoke.

He stopped short of hitting the table to shake them all into action. "They've declared war on us. Are we just going to wait until they fire another shot?"

Dax nodded. "It's no surprise that I second Jackson."

One down, five more Traubs to go, and Jackson could see by the stubborn expressions on his relatives' faces that they needed some more persuading.

He pulled out the most powerful weapon he could think of—one that wouldn't necessarily affect DJ, but one that would strike true at the hearts of his brothers and sister.

"Dad would've wanted us to stand up for family," he said, believing it with all his soul. Although he had been just a kid when his real father had died, Jackson had always lived under the impression that his dad had been noble—that he had been perfect in a lot of ways.

He would have held his children to a high, all-for-one, one-for-all standard, and Jackson had spent a lot of time trying to live up to that. And oftentimes failing.

The rest of the Traubs merely stared at Jackson, as if they couldn't believe their brother had dared bring up their father's name in this.

Dillon blew out a breath, as if it would calm down the rest of the room, too. Then he said, "None of us were really old enough to know what Dad would've wanted, Jackson. Furthermore, I doubt he would've wanted any kind of war, under almost any circumstances."

Jackson held his tongue. It could be that Dillon was right, but Jackson didn't want to admit that—it would have meant that he didn't know much about his father at all.

Rose finally said, "Why don't we ask the person who's most affected by this?" she said. "DJ? What do you think?"

Slowly, DJ rose from his chair, his body so tense that Jackson thought he might break apart any second.

"I think," he said, "that when a man is being attacked, he doesn't go forward unarmed. But—" he added "—he doesn't provoke the other side, either. There have got to be ways to counter LipSmackin' Ribs that don't include extreme measures."

Jackson realized that he had fisted his hands on the table, and he loosened them, suddenly remembering his deal with Laila.

No more kicking butt. More...sweetness... instead.

Or not so much *that* as subtlety.

As the idea permeated him, he realized that this was probably what his real dad would have truly wanted—that honor wasn't necessarily brought about by the use of fists.

Jackson just wished he knew for certain.

That same day, Laila couldn't seem to sit at her desk for more than a few minutes at a time.

She just couldn't get her mind off last night's date.

And Jackson.

She could really strangle him. One minute, he was wooing her by candlelight in the Gallatin Room, and the next they were in his truck cab, with that soft country song playing and him smelling so good and inching closer to her...

Close enough that she couldn't have said no to him about anything.

But she had lucked out in that area, she guessed. Again, he had been the one to back off what would surely have been a compromising situation in her parking lot, had any of her neighbors passed by and seen beyond the steamed-up windows. Once again, Laila had been ready for a whole lot more from Jackson than she had gotten.

How weird was it that he was actually somewhat of a gentleman when she—the supposed lady—was hardly acting genteel? Of course, she was sure that this whole act of his was designed to string her along and drive her so crazy that she would hop all over him when he finally decided to stop toying with her, but she rather liked being reeled in like this.

Or was this actually his way of *chasing* her?

For the next fifteen minutes, she did her best to work, and when she saw Mike Trudeau in the lobby, chatting with some of the tellers who didn't have customers at the moment, she finally recognized a chance to be productive.

If there was one thing that Jackson *had* given her, it was that piece of advice about kicking butt.

She smoothed down her forties-style pantsuit and tried not to think about yet another instance when her boss would shoot her ideas down or give her that look that said she was nothing more than someone who should have pursued an MRS degree in college.

Mike Trudeau had wandered over to Dana's desk, and as Laila's best friend adjusted her glasses and smiled at her boss, Laila sucked it up, stood from her chair and went out her door.

Kick butt, she kept hearing Jackson say.

She approached Dana's desk just in time for her friend to push a recalcitrant strand of taboo purple hair back into her conservative 'do before the boss noticed.

"Morning, Miss Cates," Dana said, tongue in cheek.

Mike Trudeau turned around, all grandpalike in his cable-knit sweater. "Hello, there, Laila. Happy Wednesday."

It was actually Tuesday, but Laila didn't correct him. "Morning."

"I was just telling Dana that I'm off on a trip."

Dana picked up a pencil, absently winding it

through her fingers. "A hunting jaunt for Papa Banker," she said to Laila.

"I should've guessed." Laila put on her best, most persuasive professional smile and aimed it at her boss.

Kick butt!

"Mike," she said, "is now a good time to touch base with you before you leave?"

"Well…"

Again, it was Jackson's Texas round-'em-up voice she heard saying, *Don't let him off the hook*....

Unwilling to accept no for an answer, she began walking to her boss's office. When she glanced behind her, just to see if this was working, she saw that he was surprised.

And the look Dana had on her face?

Happy as all get-out. She might as well have been pumping her fist in the air because if Laila had told Dana once about her frustrations at the bank, she had told her a million times.

She made herself right at home in his office, taking a seat, crossing one leg over the other, as polite as possible while he walked inside and waited by his desk.

Not giving him a chance to lead the conversation, she started in. "Did you have a chance to read my latest proposal?"

"I…"

She would take that as a negative.

Then she did something she never thought she would do in her life—she launched right into the nitty-gritty of her idea, selling it as she had never sold anything before.

In fact, she might have even been channeling Jackson Traub and his silver tongue.

When she was done talking about the benefits of loaning more money to the community's small businesses and homeowners, Mike Trudeau was watching her, a tiny smile pulling up the corners of his mouth.

"Why, Laila," he said, "I didn't know you had it in you."

"These ideas? I've laid them out for you more than once, Mike."

He chuckled, and she could tell he was recognizing that he had been called out.

"I like this," he said. "Go-gettedness. Now I saw enough in you to recognize that you could run a bank, but you've got a lot more going on, don't you?"

A lot more. More than a face. More than the surface.

She couldn't help but glow at that.

As her boss finally sat down and started to run some numbers with her, she didn't stop glowing.

It didn't even diminish when she got back to her office, where, for the first time in her career, she leaned back in her chair, kicked up her heels and rested her fashionable boots on the desk.

What now, though?

Even though it was a quarter to five, she didn't want to call it a day and go home. Lord Vader, swimming around in his fishbowl, wouldn't care much about her big victory today.

She thought about asking Dana to go out and celebrate, but then she remembered that her friend was going out tonight with her on-again-off-again boyfriend, a traveling salesman who was in town for a couple of days.

What about her other friends, though?

Laila went through her mental address book, only to realize that just about everyone she used to have girls'-nights-out with were married with children.

That twang of yearning blasted through Laila again as she thought of babies...and Cade telling her that maybe they could get married before it was too late.

Here she was, sitting around, not knowing who she could share her good news with. Wishing she knew Jackson well enough to just call him up and say, *"Hey—want to hang out? Want to be my friend?"*

Friend, indeed. He was nothing of the sort. He wasn't the kind of guy who would genuinely care about all her long-range plans and successes.

Puzzled that she would even want this from him, she put her feet on the floor. She knew who she could depend on, always and forever. Her family.

Wasn't it time to finally sit down and talk to Abby?

Laila opened up a desk drawer, took her cell phone out of her purse and called her youngest sister.

Abby answered on the fourth ring. "Hello?"

"Hey."

Her sister detected Laila's upbeat mood right away. "What's going on? Did you win some kind of lottery?"

Laila sighed, wanting so badly to get to the bottom of Abby's remarks. "No jackpots, just a good day at work."

"Glad to hear it."

"And I want to have some fun, too. Celebrate a minor victory with my boss. You want to go to the Hitching Post with me? My treat."

Abby's hesitation made Laila think that her sister knew there was an ulterior motive here.

"Abby," Laila said. "Come on. It'll be fun.

When's the last time I got to spend quality time with my sis?"

"It's been awhile, hasn't it?"

"Yeah." Laila was smiling. "So what do you say?"

It didn't take long for Abby to respond, and that had to be a positive sign.

"Sounds good."

"All right. I'm going to head there straight from work."

"Great. And Laila?"

"Yes?"

Abby seemed to rethink whatever she had been about to say. Or maybe she just wanted to say it when they were together.

"Nothing. I'll see you soon, okay?"

They signed off, and Laila closed her phone, more confused than ever about what she had done to her little sister to merit the standoffish treatment.

And what she could do to make whatever it was better.

Chapter 7

"Jackson," said Rose as they left Traub Oil's office building, "you'd better not be following me."

"Aw, Rose..." He was always one to take the opportunity to razz his little sis. "You know I live for dogging you during one of your dates. The minute I heard you'd be going out, I knew I'd have to sit across the room from you at the Hitching Post and make threatening faces to whoever it is you're meeting in such secrecy."

Not true. He just had a mighty yen for those burgers the Hitching Post sold and wanted to take one home. After the last meeting with the family, he had assured them that he was building up to talking to the manager at the Post one of these nights when he was in, making the case for DJ's ribs. Jackson was sure that, as a good customer and persuader in general, he might hold some sway.

Rose rolled her blue eyes just before Jackson fell behind her. With her red hair and fresh complexion, she looked much younger than thirty. For some reason, the girl had a real tough time finding the right man, and since coming to Thunder Canyon, she had become determined to discover her Mr. Perfect.

Jackson knew her mission had something to do with how the rest of his siblings seemed to be falling, one by one, to the big bad force known as love, but what was the point?

He pulled on his coat, although this evening wasn't quite as chilly as last night. "Don't worry, Rose, I'll be out of the Hitching Post before *you* have your date eating from your delicate hand."

"Oh, I'm sure he won't be that simple to win over. Besides, we only agreed to meet for drinks, so this isn't a full-blown date. I'm not sure he's ready for that yet."

"Who?"

"Cade Pritchett."

As Rose went on her merry way ahead of him, Jackson stopped in his tracks.

Pritchett?

Not only was it a surprise that Rose was meeting with the man, but what would happen when Jackson saw him at the Hitching Post? This would be the first time he would be encountering his rival for Laila's affections since he had "saved" her that one night when Cade had been having that intense conversation with her.

But since Pritchett was going out with another woman—Jackson's sister, to boot—did that mean he was over Laila?

Now Jackson wasn't just wondering if there would be any hard feelings between him and Cade—he was also wondering whether the man was going to end up breaking his little sister's heart if he was still interested in Laila.

Those were definitely good enough reasons in and of themselves to still go to the bar and grill. Yet there was also something else pushing Jackson to continue on his way there.

If his real father was looking down on him at this very moment, he might be proud not only of how Jackson was coming to terms with handling the rib war, but that he wanted to smooth things over with Cade—and he would do it while looking out for Rose as well.

Shoving his hands into his pockets, he let

his sister walk alone, trailing far enough behind her so that she would have time to settle into her date at the tavern.

When he walked into the bar area, the place was bustling with activity—waitresses fulfilling Happy Hour orders, townsfolk huddled over the bar tables, the sound of utensils and the low murmur of the jukebox.

Rose and Cade were already at a small table. When she spied Jackson, she narrowed her eyes in a "You never listen, anyway" manner, then gave an accepting wave.

Cade turned around to see who she was greeting, stiffening his spine once he saw it was Jackson.

A decent man would go right on over to say hi, to let Cade know that there was no reason to nurse any hard feelings because of the situation with Laila. More importantly, though, a decent man would let Pritchett know that he was being watched, just in case he was merely stringing Rose along.

This one's for you, Dad, Jackson thought, sauntering over to their table.

Rose greeted him first. "This is why I love small towns—no privacy whatsoever."

Jackson extended his hand to her date. "Cade."

He accepted the handshake. "Traub."

Although Pritchett offered nothing more than that, he nodded at Jackson, and Jackson got the feeling that Cade just wanted this awkwardness between them to be over and done with.

Did that mean Pritchett didn't mind that Jackson had gone out with Laila a time or two? *Had* he decided to move on?

Jackson sent a gauging look to Rose, who was clearly ready to resume the date.

"Have fun, you two," Jackson said, tipping his hat. "Not too much fun, though."

"Scram," Rose said, grinning.

Jackson chuckled, glad to see that Cade was wearing something of a grin, too.

He retreated to the bar, where there was only one space open, between an elderly cowpoke and a middle-aged man who had his back to Jackson while he drank wine with a woman Jackson guessed to be his wife.

Unfortunately, the seat was within earshot of Rose and Cade's table.

But neither of them seemed to notice Jackson with their backs to the bar, a distance between them that was roomy enough to scream *FIRST DATE* while being intimate enough to let everyone know that they were together.

After asking the bartender if the manager was in tonight—he wasn't—Jackson gave his burger order and, while he waited, he caught Rose's voice.

Maybe his attention was even snagged because of one word she uttered in particular.

"You know he's been seeing Laila," Rose said in her usual straightforward manner. "Don't you?"

Laila. Her name echoed in Jackson, reverberating, chiseling away at him in ways he had never suspected could happen.

Pritchett hesitated, as if he'd been caught off balance. But if he had hoped Rose wouldn't address the elephant in the room, he was dating the wrong girl.

"I'm aware that they've been going out with each other," Pritchett said, somewhat carefully.

"Are you still aiming to marry her?"

Jackson was riveted.

"Now, Rose…" Pritchett said.

"It doesn't mean you can't have a drink with a girl, as you're doing now. I'm only getting a sense of what's what, Cade. You can't blame me for not wanting to waste my time." She paused. "I'm not naive enough to think that you wouldn't still have some feelings for Laila, even if she turned you down."

Jackson almost felt what Pritchett must be feeling in his gut—a well-aimed punch from a well-meaning woman.

"I'm here to have fun," Pritchett finally said. "That's what you want, too, right?"

"I'm all for it. But I'm not about to embark on a date with a man whose gaze is always on the nearest doorway."

Pritchett must have had that quiet, thoughtful look on his face that Jackson had seen before, because Rose added, "*Do* you still have your sights set on Laila, even if you're here with me?"

When Cade didn't answer directly, Jackson's hackles went up—not only for his sister, but because he had earlier misjudged Pritchett. Clearly, he still carried a torch for Laila.

"Rose," he said, "the truth is that I'm a realist. And I know Laila doesn't love me, but I want to marry and have a family. I figure a good case of 'like' may be better than a passionate relationship that's doomed to burn out."

"So you're just marking time until she comes around?"

"I wish you hadn't started this conversation."

"Better now than later."

Pritchett sighed. "The bottom line is that

Laila's got a lot of common sense, and she'll get back in touch with it. No one wants to get old by themselves."

Jackson could almost picture Rose's stunned expression as Pritchett continued.

"Everyone gets tired of being alone."

Another beat passed before Rose answered. "Not *that* tired."

"Well, I'm to that point, and I've been dating Laila a good long time. If I didn't have to start over with someone else, I'd be satisfied. I don't want to wait the amount of time it takes to see if I'm compatible with a woman when I already know that's how it already is with Laila."

It was all Jackson could do not to turn around and ask if Pritchett was hoping to make Laila jealous by being seen in public with another woman. But, then again, there had been rumors Jackson had heard lately about Pritchett—something about a girlfriend who had died pretty suddenly and how he had emotionally shut down afterward.

How much did that have to do with his philosophy?

Even more confusing, why had Rose decided to go out with Cade Pritchett in the first place? Because she really *was* tired of sitting home alone?

Even though the fine hairs were raised on his arms, Jackson told himself just to sit there and not say a word. Rose was no shrinking violet, and she would have everything under control. And as far as Laila went?

Hell, he was damn sure Cade Pritchett didn't have a chance.

Pritchett offered one last comment. "I don't want to risk a life without companionship and children, Rose, and if I have to settle to get it, that's what I'll do."

"Wow," she said. "To me, a loveless marriage would be a fate worse than death."

And, with that, it seemed as if their date was over before it had even started.

Jackson peered over his shoulder to find Rose and Pritchett drinking their sodas, silent as could be. It reminded him of some of those long rides home that he had endured with Laila.

Jackson found himself smiling like a fool, just at the thought of her, and he cleared his throat.

The sound made Pritchett look back at Jackson, and from the expression on the other man's face, it seemed as if he had known that Jackson was nearby the whole time and had merely been warning off his rival by being honest about his unchanged intentions when it came to Laila.

Jackson didn't break gazes with him until the man turned back around to his drink. And when Jackson checked in with Rose, just to see if *she* was the one who needed rescuing from Cade Pritchett this time around, he noticed that his sister was watching the doorway, none the worse for wear.

A cute female whom Jackson knew to be one of Laila's sisters had walked into the Hitching Post, but in spite of the family relationship, she didn't resemble Laila all that much, with her long brown hair.

Was her name Abby?

Thing was, Abby had come to a standstill, her gaze smack-dab on a distracted Pritchett. She seemed to be realizing that he was on a date with Rose, and the look on *her* face…

Good God, was the girl head over heels for Cade Pritchett?

Jackson glanced at his sister, who had looked over at him, too, raising her eyebrow in a what-the-hell-is-going-on? gesture. She had recognized Abby's lovelorn expression right off the bat as well.

It was also obvious that Rose had already cut loose from her date with Cade.

Jackson smiled at her, and she shrugged.

Across from the bar area, Abby had found

a table and slipped into a chair. And not a few seconds later...

It was as if Jackson sensed Laila before she even entered. But when she did, the room seemed to go quiet, everything blocked out but Laila as she started to unbutton her long felt coat. She smiled at Abby and gave a little wave, tucked a wayward strand of blond hair that had escaped her barrette behind an ear and went to her sister's table.

Jackson was a whirl of conflicting emotions—a foreign, enveloping warmth creeping through him, primal heat in the places that were always affected by Laila.

A war that was forcing him to choose a side.

When he glanced away from her, telling himself that he wasn't going to cross the room to say hi—that he should stay away until he could make sense of what was happening to him—he saw that Rose had spied the look on his face, too, just as she had done with Abby.

She was wearing a wondering, surprised smile, and Jackson turned back to the bar before she could react to anything more on him.

Abby was the first person Laila had seen in the Hitching Post, and she didn't even look around before embracing her little sister.

She must have hugged her too enthusiastically because Abby laughed, then patted Laila's back as they both sat down.

"You'd think we haven't seen each other in forever," Abby said.

"I feel like we didn't get to spend much time together on Sunday." There—that was a good enough hint as to the main reason she had asked Abby here.

But as soon as Abby was in her chair again, Laila could tell that her sister was more unfocused than ever. She picked at her napkin, and there was a distance in her gaze.

"Is everything okay?" Laila asked.

"Sure."

Their waitress arrived to take their order—breaded cheese sticks, buffalo wings and pink lemonade. As the ponytailed woman left, Laila took off her coat and rested it on the back of her chair.

That was when something curious happened.

Abby snuck a peek across the room, and it was such a furtive gesture that Laila just had to take a gander in the same direction.

Cade Pritchett was sitting at a table with a redhead whom Laila knew to be one of the Texas Traubs. Rose, Jackson's sister.

Abby turned right back around, her face flushed.

Before Laila could think too much about it, her attention was snagged by a familiar sight behind Cade and Rose: broad shoulders under a brushed-twill coat she knew all too well, brown hair curling out from under a cowboy hat and over the coat's collar...

Her heart gave a painful yet enticing leap. Jackson.

As excitement swirled through her, Laila vowed to sit in her chair and not move a muscle. Dammit, after everything he had put her through, teasing her until she could barely see straight, *she* wasn't about to go up to *him*.

The waitress brought their drinks and appetizers, but Abby only played with her straw.

"Abby..." Laila said.

Her sister interrupted. "Doesn't it bother you to see him on a date?"

At first, Laila thought Abby was talking about Jackson, but when she took a second look over to where he was standing at the bar, it became obvious that he was there alone.

Alone and open for the taking, if Laila crept up behind him, slid her hands under his coat, over the muscles of his back, hearing him suck in a surprised breath as he recognized her...

Laila shook off the fantasy, determined to really listen to Abby. "Who are you talking about?"

"Cade." Even though Abby didn't say it with a lot of attitude, it somehow seemed as if Laila had offended her in some way.

"No, it doesn't bother me to see him here with another woman." Laila smiled, reaching out to touch her sister's hand, which was balled next to her drinking glass. "I'm glad Cade is getting out there again."

"It must've taken a lot for him to do it, after the way you treated him."

Gobsmacked, Laila sat back in her chair. "I never expected him to propose to me, Abby, especially the way he did."

"I'm not saying it isn't a good thing that you turned him down." She sighed, her brown eyes softening. "It's just that I feel for his hurt pride."

She said it in such a way that Laila blinked.

Did Abby...?

Was she...?

Abby had to know what was going through Laila's head, because she made an "Oh, please, don't even think it" gesture. "I've been like a little sister to him for years," she said. "Of course I'm going to be concerned about him."

Okay, that made sense. Abby and Cade did have a close relationship, so why *wouldn't* she have looked at the proposal fiasco from his side?

Just as Laila took another glance at Cade's table, Rose had finished her soda and stood up. She had put on her coat, and Cade had followed suit. They were now heading toward the door, but not before Rose squeezed Jackson's shoulder in farewell.

He touched the brim of his hat, then watched them leave. And when he glanced over his shoulder, at Laila, she knew that he had been aware of her presence in the room for a while.

With a grin, he turned back to the bar.

It was a replay of that other night, when he had been pretending not to notice her while she had sat at a table with Cade.

Laila let out a frustrated sound—something close to a "grr."

Abby was rubbing her temple with one hand. "Would you throttle me if I asked for a rain check tonight?"

"Do you have a headache?" Something was most certainly going on with Abby— maybe even more than her concern about Cade—but this didn't seem to be the night to investigate it.

Yet when would the right time come with her sister?

"My head's killing me," Abby said. "Big time."

"I don't mind a rain check at all. But Abby?"

Her sister had risen out of her seat and had her coat in hand. "Yeah?"

Laila wished they didn't have a seven-year canyon between them, wished they had been closer while growing up.

Abby seemed to be feeling the same thing, and she offered a tentative smile. "I know we need to get some things cleared up between us. I'm serious about having a good talk another time."

Just before Abby left, the sisters hugged, then Laila watched Abby go.

She was just about to sit again—only to finish her drink and snack on the appetizers, she told herself—when a deep voice sounded from just over her shoulder.

"You've got to stop following me around."

As shivers tumbled down her skin, she glanced at the bar, realizing Jackson wasn't there anymore.

Nope, he was right in back of her now, so downright handsome and appealing that her entire body was aflutter.

"I think you've got that backwards," she said. "You're hounding *me*."

"Think again." He held up a food container. "I've got an alibi—I came here to pick up some dinner."

She gestured toward the abandoned appetizers and drinks on her table. "And I don't have a good excuse to be here?"

"Box that food up and we'll find somewhere to eat together, away from here," he said, and it was with such casual demand that her chest folded in on itself.

Who was he to order her around?

Who was she to *like* it?

With a rebellious stare, she sat down in her chair. Nope—she wasn't going anywhere with him. Not that easily.

Laughing, he joined her, then just as careless as you please, propped up his boots in the chair beside her and dug into her food.

While he was making quick work of the buffalo wings, he said, "I'm sure it didn't escape your notice that Cade was here with my sister."

"I saw." She took up a cheese stick, nibbling on it, liking it when she saw that Jackson was paying quite a bit of attention to how she ate.

He seemed to realize what he was doing, grinned to himself, and took a swallow of Abby's untouched lemonade. Then he said, "They left early, Cade and Rose. I suspect he was walking her to her car, and that was the end of it."

"It wasn't meant to be."

"He's still got his hopes pinned on you, Laila."

Suddenly, the playful mood let up a little.

Jackson finished off a wing. "I overheard him talking to Rose about you."

Great. "What should I do to make him see that it's not going to happen?"

"Keep dating me." He wiped his hands on the napkin just before he went for the cheese sticks.

"And that should solve everything." Laila crossed her arms over her chest.

"Hey, you've done what you can to discourage Cade. Now you just have to live life."

She supposed he was right. "All I can hope is that he'll find someone someday."

Jackson got a mysterious gleam in his eyes. "Maybe sooner than you think."

Before she could ask him what he meant by that, he just up and left the table, throwing down way more money than the check would require and heading for the rear of the establishment, back to where she knew there were pool tables.

Did he want her to follow or something?

Well, it would be a long autumn in hell before she gave in to his wants.

Just as she was finding her spine when it came to Jackson, he paused near the back wall, leaned against it for a moment, acknowledging that she was making a big stand against him.

And when he shot that grin at her, then jerked his chin toward the back room, her veins pulled within her so violently that she felt like his puppet.

Let's call a truce, his gesture seemed to say, and Lord help her, but she was all for it.

At least she *sort of* was. She did enjoy the flirtation, the maddening frustration of butting heads with him. It made her blood race, made her feel more alive than she had in...

Well, ever.

He continued toward the back, and like the marionette she was, she grabbed her coat and purse from the back of her chair and followed.

For now.

By the time she got to the back room, he was already racking up the pool balls, and his grin told her that he had known she couldn't resist him. Jerk.

"Name the stakes," he said, hanging the racking tray back on the wall and chalking his cue stick.

"Oh, a gambler, are we?"

"I know when to hold them and when to fold them, all right."

"That's poker."

"The same basic rules apply here." He nodded toward the table, setting the chalk on the corner. "So…what are we going to bet, Miss Laila?"

Her pulse was jumping, urged on by his soft, I-dare-you tone.

"I'll bet that you're much better than I am," she said, the words barely getting out as she carefully folded her coat and purse over a nearby chair.

"You don't play?"

She offered an innocent lift of her shoulders, a liar through and through. Little did Jackson Traub know that her parents had a pool table in their rec room.

He smiled, dangerous and hardly worthy of trust. "Then I'll go easy on you."

"Oh, please do."

He spread his arm, indicating that she should shoot first. She went to the wall, grabbed the stick of her choice, then chalked the tip, acting like she barely knew what to do.

"I guess," she said, "that I should bet something small."

"Since you're gonna lose?"

"Who knows?" She sent him a saccharine smile. "You just might have an off night."

"How about this—if you lose, I get..." He seemed to think about it.

"A kiss," she said.

"I've already gotten a kiss."

And from the expression he was wearing, he had enjoyed taking it, too.

Taking every single one of them.

"Then," she said, "you'll just have to make do with another kiss. But, again, you might not win."

"And if *you* do?"

"You'll have to leave town pronto, mister."

He laughed. "Not before I throw you over my shoulder and take you with me."

The primal image dug deep into her belly, warming her—no, *heating* her. Was it just because of the sexual thrill?

Or was it because he had said he would take her with him, even in jest?

She shut the very possibility out of her mind. She would never leave Thunder Canyon, her family, her friends.

And he definitely wouldn't be staying.

The very thought gave her more courage than usual, gave her a shot of freedom to do what she wanted to do with a man who wasn't asking for a commitment.

She bent down to the table, ready to strike—and when she did, the balls scattered, two striped ones going into the pockets.

"Is it too late," she said, "to amend my bet? It already looks like you'll be leaving town with your tail between your legs after everyone hears about how you were whooped by a girl."

She felt him in back of her, one of his arms bracing her left side as he caged her by positioning the other on the right.

His voice was warm in her ear. "What kind of stakes are you thinking about now?"

Something much higher than I ever thought it would be, she thought as her heart seemed to get squeezed by an invisible fist.

"If I win," she said, turning her face so that his lips barely touched her cheek, "I—"

Before she got the next word out, he had scooped her up, bringing her to him, his mouth crushing down on hers.

Chapter 8

It all happened in such a passionate blur that Jackson barely remembered dropping his cue stick, grabbing Laila's coat and purse from their chair, then sweeping her out the back door and to the Dodge Aspen coupe she had parked nearby.

He set her down on the ground, snatched the keys from her coat pocket, unlocked the door, picked her up again, slid her over the long front seat and to the passenger's side, then took his place behind the wheel.

Then he drove until he found a tree-darkened cove on the side of some road.

There he cut the engine and she stared at

him in the breath-heavy quiet, her eyes wide, just before he dragged her onto his lap, resuming their kiss, as if they were two teenagers necking at a drive-in movie.

As she responded with just as much enthusiasm as any hormone-addled kid, he ran his mouth over her neck, her soft skin carrying the scent of a summer afternoon.

She panted. "You never did let me finish what I was going to say back at the Hitching Post."

"You aim to finish now?" he asked against her throat.

She grabbed onto his arms as he nipped at her. "Of course I want to fin—"

He raised his head. "Laila?"

"What?" A whisper. Needful.

He wanted to tell her to stop talking, to forget about the bets they had been talking about at the pool table, forget all the games they had been playing.

But instead of saying anything, he looked into her eyes, the blue of them lit by the moon shining through the car windows. He reached up, carefully unpinning her hair from the barrette that was holding it back from her face.

When her blond waves tumbled down, he sucked in a breath.

Beautiful. Damn she was so beautiful, and it wasn't just because of her hair or her face or the graceful curves of her figure.

What was it then?

And why couldn't he seem to get enough?

He shed his coat while she watched from her spot on his lap, then pushed the material into the corner of the long front seat. As if in acquiescence, she took off his cowboy hat, banishing it to the back.

Their breaths were coming in ragged rhythm now, and a flaring hunger was tearing him up from the inside out.

"Do you still want to talk about what you were going to say at the Hitching Post?" he asked.

But that wasn't what he wanted to know at all, and she seemed to realize that he was asking if they should stop now because, this time, he wouldn't be the one who would pull away, giving her some flip excuse about her thinking he was easy to get or something.

She answered by leaning down to him, pressing her mouth to his with such tenderness that he groaned a little, low in his throat.

Her lips were soft, warm, and his head got fuzzy again. At this instant, she owned him, and it should have sent him running.

Yet he stayed right here, skimming his hands down her arms, feeling the smooth fabric of her suit as it whispered beneath his fingers. He reached her hands, then her thighs, resting his palms on the sides of her legs, where her long suit jacket covered her fashionable, fitted pants.

His stylish lady.

His darling for the night.

Right now, he wanted a hell of a lot more than that, though. He wanted...

How long with her? A week?

A month?

Or...?

His mind blanked as they kissed once more, a lazy whirl of passing moments and heartbeats. He entered her mouth with his tongue, and she rocked against him, a move that could only be instinctive.

But she was obviously waiting for his cue, probably because he had teased her too much in the past, leading her on, then backing off.

Not now, though—he was at his limit.

He undid one button on her jacket, then another.

As her chest rose and fell, he gave her one more opportunity. "What were the stakes of the game going to be, Laila?"

She obviously understood his coded words, yet before she could answer, he slid his fingers into her opened jacket, feeling warm flesh, the toned lines of her waist.

"I was just going to ask for a kiss, too," she finally said.

And he gave it to her, whether she had won the pool match or not. She had already won *him* over, and that was all that counted.

Afterward, he still kept his mouth on hers, even as he sketched his hands up her waist.

"Are we square now?" he asked, coming to her breasts.

He cupped them, feeling lace, rounded softness, hearing her gasp yet again, sharper this time as she leaned back her head. The sound bolted into him, lancing and tearing, and he wanted to hear what she would do if he touched her in all the right, hidden places.

He ran his thumbs over her nipples, bringing them to pebbled nubs.

She didn't ever answer his question but, then again, he hadn't meant for her to. She only bit her lip, shifted on his lap, drove him that much more to a brink he wasn't going to come back from tonight—not if the throb of his nethers told him anything.

With deft movement, he unhooked the front

of her bra, peeling back the lace so he could see her in the moonlight.

And...dammit all. She was beautiful here, too, her breasts full, just slightly tipped up, as if begging for him to sip at them.

But he just wanted to look first. Wanted to memorize her so that, when he was gone, he could remember.

He trailed his knuckles under her breasts, shaping, his groin getting harder by the second.

"You're killing me," she said.

And she was doing the same to him.

He leaned forward, touching the tip of his tongue to a nipple. Then he did it to the other one, taking his time, making her hips wiggle as she grew even more restless.

When he thought he had tortured her enough, he took her all the way into his mouth, sucking, pressing his hands against her back to bring her even closer.

She ground her hips into him, giving as good as she was getting, finally making him draw away because all he wanted now was to have her fully against him, laid out on the seat, every inch his.

Pulling one of her legs so that she wrapped it around him, he eased her down to the cushions. He brought her hips up so that they were flush against each other, and they strained, just like those teenage kids at the drive-in, steaming up the windows again.

The steam gathered inside him as well, pulsing and pushing, tapping like a time bomb.

He couldn't take any more of this, and he reached for his coat, propping it under her head.

Her light hair spread over the brushed twill, the seat, a fall of waves that struck him hard.

His Laila.

Slowly, he reached for one of her legs, stroked his hand down the length of it until he came to the slick leather boot she was wearing. He pushed up her pant leg, pulled down the boot's zipper, the sound buzzing through the air, imitating the blood that was swarming him with heat.

After taking off her silky sock, he gave the same attention to her other leg.

Then he swept his palms to the back of her, traveling up her calves, her thighs, to her rear, bringing her up against him again as she arched and exhaled.

He found her pants zipper on the side, and he undid that, too, tossing the material to the floorboard.

Feverishly, she unbuttoned his shirt, stripping that off, fumbling with the fly of his jeans, then pushing down the denim. Pushing down her panties and getting rid of those.

As she took him in her palm, he just about exploded.

"Hold on..." He didn't even know if she understood what he had said, because it had come out so garbled. He reached into his jeans pocket, pulled out a condom, managed to unwrap it and sheathe himself.

"Oh, Jackson..."

He lifted her hips, pushing into her on a moan and, suddenly, he couldn't think any more.

All he could see were a million lights in his head, blinding him, needling him with their piercing heat. They flowed with his body as he drove into her, out again, then in, and she moved with every one of his thrusts, little sounds of delight urging him onward until those lights in his head throbbed, painful, impaling him, lifting him—

He did explode then, and he fell just as hard, his sight and mind coming back to him moment by moment, making him realize that he was holding tight to Laila, as if never wanting to let her go.

And she was holding just as tightly to him.

Jackson buried his face in her thick hair, breathing her in, thinking that he could stay this way for the rest of his life.

Afterward, they had pieced themselves back together, not saying much to each other, because what *was* there to say?

I usually don't move this fast with a man, even if I date a lot of them....

It just sounded like an excuse she didn't want to make—not while her body was still vibrating at a low, sensual hum, craving another round of him.

She never wanted this night to end.

Something inside her wondered why she should let it.

Kick butt, she thought to herself. *Why not get exactly what you want?*

Holding to those thoughts, she buttoned up her suit jacket. Jackson, who had already gotten dressed, too, turned on the car motor and it growled. Outside, tree branches left jagged silhouettes against the moon-bathed sky.

Ratcheting up her courage, she went for it. "I don't know about you, but I'm not ready to go home."

He glanced at her, coasted his fingertips over her cheek. It could have been a trick of the moonlight, but she thought she saw exposed emotion in his gaze, although she couldn't say just what that emotion was.

"Me, either," he said.

Her heart twisted, as if it was intent on going somewhere she had never been willing to venture.

But that couldn't be. Laila never fell for anyone.

Yet what if...?

No, she told herself. This was only the afterglow. She wanted more adrenaline, more excitement singing through her, that was all.

He was tracing his thumb over her cheekbone. "How about you call in sick tomorrow?"

She laughed. "I haven't called in sick for years."

"Okay." He stopped touching her. "You're right. Don't let me be a bad influence on you."

"You weren't influencing me so badly ten minutes ago."

At first, she couldn't believe she had been the one to say that, but why not? She had played it safe for so much of her life—why not invite a little game changer now? It wouldn't be a long-term thing since Jackson wasn't here to stay, anyway.

It would be a no-loss situation with so much to gain.

He was smiling at her comment. "Don't mind my saying so, Laila, but I'd like to keep influencing you."

"Then what do you say we get out of here?"

He gave her a long, serious glance. He paused like that for such a time that Laila even began to wonder if he was fighting something in himself—the same thing she was facing about getting involved with him.

But they had already gotten involved in a manner of speaking.

Way involved.

As if making up his mind the best that he could for the time being, he backed the car onto the deserted road, switching on the headlights. They lit the way ahead of them in a soft, warm glow as the bushes and trees and fences passed by.

It didn't take long for her to come to the conclusion that he was taking her to his rented condo up at the Thunder Canyon Resort.

Once they were inside his place, she surveyed the surroundings: leather furniture, glass tables, framed nature pictures on the walls. Modest for an oil man, but that was Jackson, in spite of how much flash his smile held.

He seemed to guess that she was thinking this wasn't a reflection of him—not a true one.

"You can get anything at the resort. The concierge arranged for a decorator to rustle up a few items to make me feel at home."

"Ansel Adams?" she asked, stopping in front of a famous black-and-white photo of the mountains in Yosemite.

"If I've got to decorate, why not?"

She gave him a curiosity-filled glance.

"Okay," he said, hanging his coat and hat on a rack near the doorway. "So I like his stuff. He's got a way of making me calm down when I need to. My ranch house has recently benefited from his pictures."

So she *was* seeing a side of him that she hadn't anticipated.

She liked imagining Jackson at home, relaxing in his house, then going outside each dawn to ride a horse, work in the stables while the sweat glistened on his skin. She liked thinking of how he would shower off all that work-earned perspiration.

A zing flew through her. She had felt the sweat on his arms and chest and everything else not so long ago, and she was dying to feel it again.

"It's a gentleman's ranch," he said, breaking into her wicked musing. "That only means it's basically a hobby. I go there on weekends, live in the city closer to the Traub Oil Texas offices the rest of the time."

"So it's like a sanctuary?"

He had been sauntering over to her, and now he eased her coat off with breath-suspending deliberation. Her skin came alive under the slip and slide of material, under the sensation of his fingers trailing down her arms.

"I guess it's just like that," he said, his voice low and scratchy. "Maybe someday you can see it."

As soon as he uttered it, she thought that he might have regretted doing so, because he turned away from her, taking her coat and hanging it next to his on the rack.

Had he been overcome by what had happened tonight? Had he spoken before he had thought twice about inviting her to what he thought of as his private retreat?

Joy raced inside her, just at the notion that he might be feeling the same way she was—scarily head over heels, willing to test what might be between them.

He laughed, and all of a sudden, she doubted that she was on the same page as he was.

"Now that I think about it," he said, "I've never brought a woman to the ranch."

"I get it, Jackson." It might be time to lighten this up. "It's your man cave."

"Doesn't every guy have one?"

"My dad does. He needs a break every so often, too. Sometimes he'll go to a cabin near his favorite fishing hole. He keeps telling us kids that, when we retire, he'll take us with him, but not a minute before."

"My own father had a retreat. My real dad." Jackson's brown gaze grew darker. "Mom said he liked to go hunting every so often. I think he might've had a cabin in the woods, just like your father, but I'm not sure if that's something I made up about him or if it's real."

Sensing that the vulnerable part of Jackson was just below the surface, she walked closer to him. It was probably a safe guess that he didn't show this side to many people, and she wanted to be a part of this while she could, while she was still feeling close to him.

She rested her hand on his arm. "You miss him, even though you didn't really know him."

He nodded. "There are times when I imagine he's still watching me and my brothers and sister from the Great Beyond, and he might be a little disappointed in what he's seeing. In me, at least."

"Every son wants to make his dad proud."

Jackson didn't say any more, as if he could cover up what he had already shared. But so much about him had already come together for her: how his commitment-shyness might just stem from his never wanting to have his heart broken again, just as it had been when his dad had died. How he might even be running for his life with *her,* even if he had shown her much differently earlier tonight.

She brushed her fingers over his cheek, then turned his gaze back to hers. "You have so much going for you, Jackson. I hope, even when you're back in Texas, you remember that."

Something expanded in his pupils, the black of them opening up.

Another release of emotion?

It could very well have been, because he cupped her jaw with his hands, leaned down to her, kissed her with such passion and force that she wondered if he was trying to forget that he was going to go back to that gentleman's ranch in Texas all too soon.

Hours later, predawn slipped through the curtains in Jackson's bedroom, casting a slice of murky light over the woman in bed next to him.

Laila was still sleeping, his covers pulled up

to her chest, one of her arms flung over her head, her hair fanned over his pillow.

A stray emotion cuddled up to Jackson, and it felt as if it had been lost for years, just coming home now.

But it couldn't be...*that*. The L-word. It made no sense, because love didn't fit into his world, wouldn't ever fit in. He just didn't have room for it.

Then again, he had sure acted as if love was in the cards last night, when he had told Laila entirely too much about himself. That seemed to happen a lot with her, though.

As he watched her in the dim light, a memory tried to push the comforting feeling away from him: a vague recollection of his mom just after Dad had died—a flash of her sobbing at his funeral. Then another piece of the past: an image of Mom sitting in her car in the driveway while Jackson looked out the window with his twin, Jason, waiting for her to come in. It had taken her what seemed like hours, even though it had to have only been a fraction of that before Dillon and Ethan had gone out to bring her inside.

Even now, Jackson's heart hurt for her. It hurt for him, too, as well as for his siblings. They had all been roughed up by their dad's death.

So why was he thinking of that now?

Needing something to make him feel better, he concentrated on what he always seemed to concentrate on when he needed it the most—the beautiful, temporarily-his woman next to him.

He traced a finger down Laila's nose, her chin, to her jaw, where he lightly tickled her.

Sleepily, she shrugged, batting his hand away.

He laughed, and she opened her eyes.

"Obviously," she said, her voice kittenish, "I'm not used to being woken up by some-one—especially if he's a self-appointed alarm clock."

Nestling an arm over her, he lay back down. "Just how many someones have there been?"

There—that would inject some much-needed reality into this morning after.

She blushed.

"Oh, come on," he said, pulling her closer to him. "I, of all people, won't judge."

"It's different for men. You can sleep with as many women as you want and nobody will think twice about it. I've always held my cards close to my chest, especially in Thunder Can-yon." She pushed back a hank of disheveled hair. "It'll be bad enough if anyone sees your truck still parked in town and wonders why you never made it home."

"They won't know I'm with you."

"They'd have to be blind to avoid that conclusion."

"Then I'll tell you what—you can get your car out of my garage and back home before dawn fully breaks and I'll call a ride to take me to the office today."

She lifted an eyebrow. "My—you're good at arranging these things."

"What can I say?" He snuck a hand under the covers, over her belly, and she gasped. "I know what I'm doing."

He tickled her again, and she squealed softly.

"I'm going to torture any information that I want out of you," he said.

"Okay, okay!" Then she smacked his hand. "Two. There have been just two men I've…"

"Loved?"

As she hesitated, his chest seemed to split open. He didn't like knowing that she'd had feelings for other guys.

"I wouldn't say love, really," she said. "I might have thought I was close to it at the time, but it turned out that it was just a couple of false alarms. Still, those instances were the nearest I've ever gotten."

She flushed again, glancing at him, then away.

He didn't want to wonder what she was really talking about, if she was thinking about what she felt for *him*.

"Anyway," she continued, "by most standards, I haven't been around the block much. The last time I was with a man, he was a consultant at the resort—an architect. I thought we were going places until we weren't."

"You realized that what you felt for him wasn't love." He had enjoyed saying that a little too much.

"Yeah, and afterward I was sure I'd never be capable of it." Her gaze went wistful. "And before that, my very first time was in college, senior year. He was a football player. Quarterback."

"Doesn't that figure?" He could have guessed that the beauty queen and the homecoming king would have gravitated toward each other, just as they did in most high schools or colleges.

"It's true—we were such a walking cliché." She pulled the covers up to her collarbone, turning toward him. "But the same thing happened with Quarterback Jeffrey—I cooled off in our relationship before…"

"…You could commit."

She nodded, touched his chin with her fingertips, as if to feel the scratch of his five o'clock shadow. "You would know that story well enough."

"What have I been telling you? We're two of a kind."

He smiled at her, and when she did the same, his pulse quickened.

"Know what?" she asked.

"What?"

"I just thought you asked me out because you'd set your cap for the local beauty queen. You were adding to your collection of conquests."

Shame nicked him, and his first instinct was to skirt the truth. Why hurt her unnecessarily? They would have had enough of each other by the time he left Montana, so why rush a breakup along?

Besides, he didn't feel that way now, and he didn't want her to know how much of an ogre he had been.

"Don't say that, Laila. The first time I saw you, there was…" Something. He rushed on, refusing to think about it too much. "I saw a spark in you, a flame…there are probably a hundred different names for what attracts one person to another."

"Right." She said it as if she hadn't expected him to get deep on her, and that tore at him a bit. "Maybe we were intimate in another life, and you saw the reflection of my reincarnated soul in my limpid gaze...."

"Cute."

Her eyes got that look that told him things were about to go back to square one, with her running and him chasing.

But he had already left all that behind.

"Laila, I just want to see you again. No more cat-and-mouse games, no more silliness. I want to be with you every day and every night while I can."

She absorbed his candid statements, then whispered, "A fling. That's what they call it, right? Something discreet?" Her voice broke a little. "Temporary?"

He didn't want to hear the rest, didn't want to face the decisions he would have to make someday—not while she was so soft and warm next to him now. Not while he could believe, just for the moment, that there was something here with Laila that he couldn't live without.

He put an end to the conversation by kissing her, and as she melted in his arms, he forgot the definition of *temporary* altogether.

Chapter 9

Days passed, forcing Laila to always look forward to the nights, when she could leave work and be with Jackson.

He was her addiction of choice right now, and she kept taking him in large doses.

The fact hadn't been lost on Dana, either, and when Laila got home from work tonight, her best friend called her on it over the phone.

"Where did you go so fast today?" Dana asked.

Laila was getting ready for Jackson, who usually dropped in near seven o'clock with take-out dinner—a habit that had formed all too quickly, with Laila barely even realizing it had happened.

The ritual might have given her second, third and fourth thoughts about seeing him if she hadn't known that their relationship was just a fleeting thing.

A fling.

Wrestling away a dull ache in her chest, she tucked her cell phone between her shoulder and ear while buttoning the roomy red sweater she had cuddled into. "I only came straight home, Dana."

"You've been taking off like a shot from work a lot lately." Her friend sounded a bit pouty.

"I've just been...busy."

A knowing chuff. "I'm going to assume it's not because you're putting in extra hours at your kitchen table on your proposal that Mr. Trudeau is developing now. Jackson's the reason."

Caught.

And it wasn't as if Laila and Jackson had made a spectacle of themselves in public. They had been lying low, basically because neither of them wanted their families to start believing they had some big deal going on.

Nonetheless, Laila couldn't fib to her best friend about her undercover liaison. "You're right," she said, going downstairs. "It's Jackson. But keep it quiet, okay?"

"Oh."

Laila didn't like the sound of that "Oh."

"I mean," Dana said, "I'm just kind of surprised you're seeing him exclusively."

She halted at the bottom of the stairs. "Why?"

"When Laila Cates goes out with a guy… Let's just say you've never been as busy as you are right now."

Busy.

What the heck did that mean?

"If you're saying that I'm so into Jackson that I'm ignoring everyone else in my life, that's not true." Laila wasn't *That Girl*.

Dana just laughed, as if she knew much better.

Laila rolled her eyes. *This* was exactly why she and Jackson weren't shouting out their fling—because everyone would assume there was much more going on than there was in reality.

"Just have fun tonight, Laila," Dana said. "I'll see you when I see you."

"Wait…" The *busy* comment was bothering her because she had always disliked it when her own friends seemed to disappear into RomanceLand when things got hot and heavy with a man. "Let's do lunch over the weekend. Saturday, noon, at the Tottering Teapot?"

"All right." And Dana was appeased. "Say hi to Jackie Boy."

"I will."

After hanging up, it wasn't long before Jackson arrived, pizza box in hand when she met him at the door.

"I had a yen for some pepperoni," he said, strolling on in as if he was already comfortable in her apartment.

Somehow, she didn't mind that. And she would have if any other man had done that.

Busy, she thought. *Am I?*

He kissed her hello, sending her blood pumping.

"You're quiet tonight," Jackson said.

She shook her head, afraid to answer, because if she began to talk about what was gnawing at her, it would become an issue. And that was why she liked seeing Jackson— because, with him, there were no issues, just good times.

He looked down at her for a moment longer, then kissed her again, slower and sultrier this time, as if he could chase away whatever was troubling her.

As always, she was putty in his hands, leaning into him, feeling as if she would be content never to come out of a kiss with Jackson Traub.

He smoothed back her hair, leaned his forehead against hers. "All better now?"

"Life is wonderful."

She smiled, and off he went to the kitchen, again, just as if it was his. But she was actually grateful for his casualness—it reminded her of what they were to each other…and it wasn't anything serious.

Once more, Dana's voice came back to Laila. *Busy…*

Laila joined him in the kitchen, getting plates and napkins while he doled out the pizza slices. Soon everything was back to the way it should be with them, with her and Jackson flopping onto the couch, getting ready for some relaxing in front of the TV.

Companions—two people who just delighted in being with each other, no strings attached.

He cast a look to Lord Vader's bowl, where the fish was puttering around.

"Wouldn't you rather have a dog?" Jackson asked.

"I'd love one, but Lord Vader is more my speed."

"Because he or she ignores you?" He cocked an eyebrow. "That trick always does seem to work with you."

She smacked his arm because he had the gall to refer to all the times he had played it cool in the Hitching Post, only to stoke her interest.

He laughed. "It's just that dogs are the best pets of all. I've got a few on my ranch."

She had been about to bite into her pizza but didn't. "Are they pet dogs? Or do they help on the ranch?"

"I've got both kinds, and I'm the one who likes to take care of them when I'm there. You know what they say about dogs being man's best friend. It's true."

Laila still couldn't wrap her mind around this. "*You* have actual pets."

"Yeah, why wouldn't I?"

Um, because he was the last person on earth who seemed interested in being any kind of caregiver?

"It's just…" She laughed. "So very paternal of you, Jackson. I never would've guessed."

"Now you don't have to."

He took his bite of pizza, having no idea that he had just tilted her world off its axis. He had been wrong about one thing when he had described himself to her early on—he *could* commit.

She tried not to let it matter, but damn, it did. Because, as it turned out, it wasn't that he couldn't bring himself to care for someone—it was that he had already made a choice not to care for her.

But when had he ever promised anything more?

When had she come to expect it?

Not liking where her thoughts were going, she turned on the TV with the remote. Courtroom drama filled the screen, the volume low.

"Good old *Judge Judy,*" Jackson said.

Laila, whose stomach had tied itself into knots, put her pizza aside. At least the TV would keep him from asking her if she was okay again.

"I watch her every weeknight," Laila said. "I was raised on this program—it's my mom's favorite." She even remembered how Mom had always made a point of getting dinner on the table and done with before *Judge Judy* came on. "Mom always loved how Judge Judy wields her brainpower."

Had her tone of voice given Jackson some kind of hint about her present, wistful mood? Had he done the math and multiplied that with the quiet way she had greeted him at the door?

He had put aside his pizza as well, so she thought that maybe he had seen past all her joking tonight.

Dang, his ability to sense her moods got to her.

But wouldn't it be nice to have a man around who balanced a little sensitivity with testosterone?

Just thinking about it sent a pointed longing through Laila—a yearning she couldn't afford.

As he rested his hand over hers, she thought it might be a good time to ease his mind and let him know that she wouldn't complicate their time together with deep emotions.

"Mom always did tell me," she said, "that brains come before beauty. I took that to heart. I made my successes in life top priority because I knew that what I built for myself would always be more solid than what someone else could give me."

"Are you explaining why you're not going to fall in love with me, Laila?"

He had said it kiddingly, but it was obvious that he got the gist of what she was trying to do.

For a second, it seemed as if he was just as baffled about what was happening with them as she was, that he was about to get all serious on her again.

Then he pulled out that patented charm-touched grin of his and lightly tugged on her hair.

"Darlin'," he said, "if there were two more

unlikely people to fall in love in this universe, I'd be hard-pressed to discover them."

It should have made her breathe easier, but instead, it felt as if all the oxygen in her lungs had been punched out.

Nonetheless, she grinned right back at him, showing him that she was fine with what they had…even if she was starting to suspect that she wasn't.

What the hell am I doing?

Jackson asked himself that for about the hundredth time as the Saturday afternoon sun struggled through a bank of clouds. The light barely touched on the Halloween-painted windows of the Tottering Teapot, where Laila had told him the other night that she would be meeting Dana for lunch.

He was sitting in his truck outside, thinking that he would surprise her by picking her up and spiriting her off to a day of driving through the country before the autumn leaves deserted the tree branches for their winter bareness. When he had made up his mind to do this, he hadn't realized that he was doing a very boyfriend-type thing.

Hell, they had woken up together in his bed

this morning. Shouldn't he have had his fill of her just from that?

Nope—not from the way his body was going through withdrawal, as if she somehow nourished him in a way that nothing or no one else could.

He recalled what he had said the other night to her about how they were the two least likely people ever to fall in love. And dammit all: As soon as he had uttered it, the comment had struck him as a downright lie.

Across the street, Laila came out of the Tottering Teapot with Dana, whose long, sandy hair sported a vivid purple streak near the back and whose off-the-wall clothing resembled something a Brit might have worn back in the days when Madonna had first hit the scene. But all Jackson really saw was Laila, with her blond hair in a low side braid. She was dressed in a striking gold cashmere sweater and a pencil-straight plaid skirt with knee-high boots.

Just that easily, Jackson's heart was dust.

She hugged Dana goodbye and spotted Jackson in his truck, waving to him with a beaming smile, then crossing the street.

With every step, his heartbeat got that much louder, overtaking him.

He got out, going around to open her door.

Aware that many pairs of curious eyes were on them, he ushered her inside without making a big lovey-dovey production of it. If she noticed, she didn't seem to mind.

Two of a kind, he thought again—except maybe Laila had a foolproof heart, something he had also thought he possessed.

Girding himself, he climbed back inside, where the scent of her had already infused the air.

"I didn't know you would be here," she said.

"I was in the neighborhood." Total bullcrap. "How was lunch?"

"Chatty, fun. Very girly."

"Do I want to hear just how girly?"

"For the most part, no." Laila folded one leg over the other as she faced him. "We talked about Dana's dating life. Then, while we were still on the subject of men, she asked if Cade had pushed his wedding agenda on me lately and I told her no."

"Maybe he's come to the realization that you weren't just putting him off about getting hitched. You were giving him the straight truth."

"I hope so. Dana thought that he's finally getting the hint because I'm still hanging out with you."

Was that what they were doing—hanging out?

Jackson shifted in his seat. She hadn't exactly invited him over to meet the parents or anything. He supposed that when that happened, it would be a red flag, and that was when he would start to worry.

"What else did you two talk about?" he asked.

"Oh, just you. Dana's as curious as anyone about *the* Jackson Traub."

"And what did you tell her?"

Laila hesitated just long enough to make him think that she wasn't going to let him know.

"I told her that I'm having the time of my life." She ran a finger over the back of his hand, which was resting on the seat.

Pricks of yearning invaded him, and he tried to hold them off.

It was as if she was the one who was playing hard to get today, and she put her hand in her lap, seeming so far away from him.

"We also talked about work," she said. "How my proposal is coming along, all that."

"Kicking butt at that bank now," he said with a sly grin that let her know he had something else to add to the discussion besides.

"What're you grinning about?"

"I don't know, but it might have something

to do with being inspired by that 'kick butt versus sweetness' deal we made."

"Do tell."

Shrugging, he said, "I think I've come up with a way to do my job and help DJ with the Rib Shack at the same time."

"Yeah?"

"Yeah." His smile grew. "Since my job is to do community outreach, I've been intending to have an open meeting or two to help educate everyone about the oil shale project. But with the way business is going for DJ, we also need to get the community behind *him.* So why not combine the two goals? Why not host some town halls where the locals can be informed *and* be treated to DJ's ribs? It'll be good promotion for both of us."

Laila crept her hand back across the neutral zone to where his was still resting on the seat, and she clasped hers over his. Warmth suffused him from fingers to toes.

"That's a really great idea, Jackson," she said.

She didn't voice it, but from the look on her face, she was also thinking about how his family would be proud that he had found a way around brute force with LipSmackin' Ribs. About how, if his father were around, he would be busting his buttons, too.

He turned his hand over, holding hers, and they stayed like that.

Just the two of them.

They were only interrupted by a soft ding from Laila's cell phone.

She ignored it, but he nodded to her purse, somewhat relieved. Saved by the bell from having something like hand-holding mean a lot more than it should.

"Go ahead," he said, reaching for the ignition and starting the truck.

"It's just a text message," she said, looking at the phone screen. "From Dana. She says that she just drove by and we're still sitting here in the truck. Then there's some cheeky speculation that I'm not even going to repeat."

"Leave it to Dana." As the engine idled, he glanced out the window, his gaze latching onto a man strolling down the walk, his hands stuffed into his blue jeans pockets, his large silver buckle catching what was there of the sunlight.

Jackson also took in the ranch hand's mustache, recognizing him yet again from the Hitching Post and the Rock Creek Diner.

"Who's that?" he asked, gesturing toward the cowboy.

She looked, then said, "Duncan Brooks."

The cowboy had spotted Jackson and Laila in the truck, and he slowed his steps, paying too much attention, setting Jackson on edge.

"And just who is Duncan Brooks?"

"Drive and I'll tell you."

Jackson gunned the accelerator, and when he glanced in the rearview mirror, he saw that the ranch hand was still watching them.

"You were saying?" Jackson asked.

Laila held up her hands while shrugging. "He's had a thing for me for a while. Shy, soft-spoken guy, works on Bo Clifton's ranch. I've never encouraged him."

"Just one of your army of admirers, huh?"

"What—are you afraid of a little competition?"

She laughed, and he did, too. But he was remembering how Duncan Brooks had been at that lunch counter the day Jackson had stupidly told DJ that he had been attracted to Laila because of her looks and that, once he left Thunder Canyon, she would be out of sight, out of mind.

The first town hall meeting for Traub Oil Montana's Bakken Shale project came a week later.

Laila wandered around one of the large tents that had been erected outside of DJ's Rib

Shack, which was connected to the Thunder Canyon Resort. The meeting had already adjourned, and it had featured a presentation by Austin Anderson about his ideas for environmentally sound oil extraction and how Traub Oil's business could benefit the community. Now the citizens who hadn't gone next door to the food tent for DJ's ribs were milling around, talking to Austin, Ethan Traub and Jackson near the front.

She took a moment to watch Jackson, who was wearing a sharp suit today. And, yow. He wore it well, even with his cowboy hat.

But what impressed her even more was how he listened so attentively, how he seemed to know the way to ease the fears about change among those who had come to the meeting with questions.

Had he gone from a rebel to a more solid man during his time in Thunder Canyon?

She noticed how Ethan stood by his brother's side, a subtle grin on his face. Even a proud one, if Laila said so.

It warmed her that Jackson could stand tall with his successful siblings now. Oddly, his success meant as much to her as her own…

A man's voice broke into her thoughts.

"He did real well."

Laila turned to find Corey Traub standing nearby, watching Jackson, too.

Tall, with light brown hair and brown eyes, Corey seemed just as satisfied with Jackson as Ethan was. "You've been a good influence on him, Laila."

She should have been used to blushing by now—Lord knows she had been doing it enough since Jackson had come to town—but here she was again, fighting the heat on her face.

"He did this all by himself," she said. "I've got nothing to do with it."

Corey gave her an amused glance. "So you say."

When Laila caught sight of her neighbor, Mrs. Haverly, approaching from the left, Corey squeezed her arm and wandered off.

Mrs. Haverly wasn't alone—she was accompanied by a towering plate of free ribs as well as Joelle Vanderhorst, a silver-haired, hoity-toity woman who was known far and wide in Thunder Canyon as a cutting gossip.

Wonderful.

Mrs. Haverly was as sweet as pie when she greeted Laila. "Your boyfriend sure puts on a good meeting."

Her boyfriend?

Had Mrs. Haverly been keeping track of Jackson going in and out of Laila's apartment?

Double wonderful.

Laila didn't bother to tell Mrs. Haverly that *boyfriend* didn't describe what Jackson was to her. "I'll tell my friend you said so. He'll be pleased."

The older woman didn't react to the innocuous description; she merely chowed down on the ribs as Joelle stood there with her arms crossed.

"Your 'friendship' with him is very surprising," she said to Laila.

Before Laila could think better of engaging in conversation with the biggest town busybody, the woman added, "Who thought you would take up with a stranger as opposed to one of the local boys who spent so much effort courting you over the years?"

"I'm sorry, Mrs. Vanderhorst," Laila said. "I didn't realize my life was up for analysis."

The woman put a hand to her chest, obviously affronted. Mrs. Haverly chuckled, her mouth ringed with rib sauce.

"I'd take up with that Jackson Traub," she said.

At least Laila's horny neighbor was on her

side, and Laila sent her a grateful smile just before excusing herself.

Who cared what any of the others thought?

It bothered her more that *she* cared so much that there was a stinging ache inside that wouldn't go away, no matter how hard she tried to chase it off.

As Jackson shook hands with Theo Cushing, a small business owner who had asked a few questions about the Bakken Shale that had been answered today, he kept an eye on Laila across the tent.

She had retreated to a corner of it, near the beverage table, where she was pouring herself a cup of water. For some reason, after she had left Mrs. Haverly and the stately older woman who had joined them, her shoulders had gone stiff and she seemed...

Bothered?

He was about to go to her when Mike Trudeau, Laila's boss at the bank, approached Jackson. Ethan shifted his position so he could check in on the conversation that Austin was having with a science teacher from the high school.

Trudeau shook Jackson's hand with hearty enthusiasm. "Fascinating stuff you've brought to us today. Thank you for it."

"Just be sure to go next door for some of those ribs," Jackson said. "DJ's are the best."

"I can't disagree with you there. The wife won't let me within a mile of that other place." He was obviously talking about LipSmackin' Ribs. "She says it's terribly lacking in class."

Good to know that they had an ally in this prominent businessman.

Then Trudeau glanced across the room, to where Jackson's gaze had strayed again.

To Laila. Always Laila.

"She's really quite a woman," the older man said.

"Yes." Jackson felt the same pull toward her that he always did. "She is."

"Yup, those pretty ones are sure great to have around. Laila's the jewel in our bank's crown, if you ask me. I suspect we have a good many customers who come in just to look at her."

Jackson bristled. Was this man insinuating that he took Laila for granted? Or even that he had given her promotions and entertained her proposals for all the wrong reasons?

"I hope I'm wrong," Jackson said, doing everything he could not to let his dander rise and take over. "But it sounds as if you don't take her all that seriously, even if she brought you a hell of an idea recently."

Trudeau seemed to realize he had misspoken. "No, no—she did bring a damn good idea to me this time. I was just saying—"

"That she's pretty." This man had pushed a button in Jackson because he knew how much it hurt when people took Laila only at face value. Jackson also knew how much her boss's comments would bruise her if she were privy to them.

It probably even mattered that Jackson was trying to make up for having said something just as stupid himself, to DJ, at that diner.

As Trudeau started looking as if he wished he could take everything back, Jackson told himself to calm down.

To keep following Laila's advice about mellowing the kick-butt attitude.

"Just so you know," he said to her boss, keeping his voice friendly, "Laila's more than a jewel in a crown. She might glitter real nicely, but her value comes from what's beneath that sparkle."

He had said it with such emotion that Trudeau's gaze had gone soft, as if he was seeing something about Jackson that even *he* wouldn't acknowledge.

But it was clear now—clear for all the world to see.

Jackson Traub was…in love.

Trudeau patted Jackson on the upper arm, and it seemed at first to be because he was apologizing. Yet there was also an admission there, man-to-man, one guy who had recognized that the other had spoken in defense of his woman.

Trudeau left, but Ethan, who was standing next to Jackson again, had apparently heard everything.

He leaned over to whisper in Jackson's ear. "Another Traub bites the dust, huh? Weren't you the one preaching against matrimony at Corey's wedding?"

Jackson cursed under his breath, then said, "It's strictly casual between me and Laila."

"And *that's* strictly BS," Ethan said.

Unfortunately, Jackson didn't have much of an argument, especially when he saw Laila across the tent looking at him, then glancing away as if she didn't want to be caught in the same impossible place he had found himself in.

Chapter 10

After the town hall meeting, Laila had taken a seat inside the open, three-story-high lobby of the resort's main lodge. It seemed that business had picked up today, thanks to the event, and people milled around the freestanding fireplace as well as the life-sized elk statue.

She had come in here, where warmth from the fireplace toasted the area, to wait for Jackson, and her nerves were wavery as she waited for him to arrive. She had seen her boss, Mike Trudeau, talking to him, and it looked as if Jackson had gotten upset for some reason. Also, he had kept glancing over at Laila, which only added to her suspicions that they had been chatting about her.

Had Jackson even been *defending* her because of something her misogynistic boss had said?

Her heart beat like delicate wings at the thought of Jackson being her knight in white armor. Yet his behavior didn't sound like it belonged in any "fling." It almost felt as if the rules were changing on Laila, and she didn't know what would be coming next.

Heck, she didn't even want to know what the conversation had been about, and she didn't want to ask.

Her phone dinged, and she checked it to find a text from her sister, Jazzy.

Mom and Dad are requesting the presence of you and Mr. Jackson Traub at Football Day tomorrow. Be there or you're on your own for birthday cake, missy!

Laila kept staring at the screen. She had nearly forgotten that, the day after tomorrow, she would be turning the big 3-0. All this running around with Jackson had kept her mind off it and, for that at least, she was grateful.

But…an invitation from her family to bring

Jackson to Football Day? No matter how much he and Laila had been trying to keep everything on the down low, their efforts clearly hadn't paid off if her family thought it was time for him to meet them.

The ultimate sign of commitment, she thought. *Meeting the parents....*

"What does that text say that's so interesting?" It was Jackson, sitting down beside her on one of the leather sofas that decorated the lobby.

Laila angled her cell away from him so he wouldn't see the invitation on the screen, but as she ran her gaze over him, she felt a sighing thaw—the realization that she actually *wanted* Jackson to come with her to her family's. That, in spite of her grand public announcement at the Miss Frontier Days pageant, she *Might. Like. To. Be. Married.*

To him.

Someday.

How hopeless was that, though?

A sense of sorrow welled up in her. Leave it to Laila Cates, single girl extraordinaire, to fall hard—and for the most entrenched bachelor on earth at that.

As Jackson tipped back his hat and gave her a smile—not a charming grin but a *real* smile that dug way down into her heart—she fell for him that much more.

What if she was wrong about him wanting to be a bachelor for the rest of his days? Was it too much to hope that, like her, he had undergone a profound change in such a short time?

Now she *wanted* to know, so she sucked up her courage and showed him the screen of her phone.

He read it, his expression impartial as he leaned back against the sofa, carelessly stretching his arm along the top of it.

When he spoke, he had reverted back to that amused tone that made her wonder what she had been thinking when she had questioned whether or not he was capable of change.

"It seems," he said, "that I'm being summoned."

"That's fair to say." She eased back against the cushions as well, training her gaze on the comers and goers walking from one end of the lobby to the other, feeling Jackson's arm against her upper back, loving the sturdy sensation of him against her, even though she knew it was fleeting. He had reminded her of their temporary situation with the way he had reacted to that text.

So she protected herself, falling into the

same flirty groove that had always defined them. The safe way.

"You should consider yourself lucky," she said. "My parents' house is something of a sanctuary for me. You'd be the first 'companion' of mine to breach Football Day."

"Are you telling me that your parents' house is like my ranch…or a cabin in the woods?"

"Just like either of them."

As he toyed with the hair at her nape, she nearly fizzed into a pool of contentment. She almost wished tomorrow and Football Day—or any other part of real life—would never arrive, just allowing them to sit here, never minding what would eventually come down the road for them.

A few people glanced over at them, but who cared if she and Jackson looked like a couple right now? They had been fooling themselves for a while, thinking they could hide what was going on between them—to avoid all the expectations being "together" would bring.

Why not live for the moment while they could?

Her heart felt heavy as he asked, "Why haven't you ever invited a date to your family's house, Laila?"

"Because the ranch is off limits on Football Day. It's a time I've only shared with my sisters, Mom, and my dad and brother. It's a separate little world."

"And you've never wanted all your worlds to collide."

"There was no reason for them to. I'm pretty good at compartmentalizing."

"I have been, too."

She noted the use of past tense, felt them both getting in deeper.

He said, "What happens when your brother and sisters bring people over?"

"*Nobody* has ever shattered the walls of Football Day. My sisters have invited guys for dinner on Saturday night so they could meet my parents, but the entire family hasn't been there."

So why was *Jackson* being summoned in front of the whole family? Laila reached for a reason. "I'll bet they invited you tomorrow because of the birthday thing. See, I made them promise that they wouldn't make a big deal of my thirtieth, so we agreed we would just eat some cake tomorrow and that would be it. Everybody's even going to give me presents on their own. I'm sure they want to include you because they think…"

She trailed off.

But he knew what she had been about to say.

"They think that, no matter what you've told them, we're serious about each other."

Laila exhaled, and he stopped playing with her hair.

"It'd be a lot of fun if you came over," she said, "but please don't feel that you have to."

She hadn't meant to say it dismissively. Had she done so because she was getting ready for him to bug out of the invitation, anyway?

He cupped her head, pressed it toward him, spoke into her ear, stirring her hair. "But they're serving birthday cake, Laila. Is there a human being in existence who'd say no to that?"

Leave it to Jackson to inject some levity.

"My big, bad birthday," she said. "I guess you should be there to see it run me over like a semi."

He kept his mouth against her head, just above her ear, and it felt so natural, so right, that she went on talking.

"I used to laugh about the whole idea of being nervous about aging. Why care? *Who* cares? That's what I used to think, anyway."

His steady embrace told her it *was* okay. "I heard your Miss Frontier Days speech, so I have an inkling of what your thirtieth birthday means to you. Everyone else in town might think that

Laila Cates has the big, bad birthday under control, but most women wouldn't go out of their way to compete in a pageant to prove a point about how being older means being better."

"It was a real silly thing to do." Then she went a step further, telling him more than she had ever told anyone else. "It was even vain."

"It was human." He took her chin between his fingers, turned her face toward him, so that she was looking into his dust-devil-colored eyes. Now, though, it seemed there was calm there, a settling.

"It's just like you said at the pageant," he murmured. "You're getting better with every day. And I imagine that'll extend to every year, as you learn new things, gain new experiences."

Like this one with him?

Would she be older but wiser after *they* parted ways?

"How would you know that I've improved when you just met me a short time ago?" she asked.

He lifted his eyebrows. "You've grown on *me* every day."

She was a mess by now—in a good way. A whipped-up, stirred-up storm of affection.

Not wanting to torture herself any more, she conjured a smile, moving on.

"Really," she said. "You don't have to suffer through pink cake and a truly terrible rendition of the birthday song at Football Day. I grant you a reprieve, Jackson Traub."

He laughed softly, kissed her on the temple.

She pulled back from him, scanning his expression. Today might have been the first time they had acted like this in public, but from the intensity in his brown eyes, she was certain that he had done it without regret.

Did he care for her more than she knew?

"Listen," he said. "I suspect that your family is real curious about the guy you've been spending so much time with, and I have no reservations about going over there with you and showing them that I hold no threat in taking away your title."

"Title?" Somehow, she doubted that he was talking about Miss Frontier Days.

Jackson laughed. "You know that one you wear so proudly? Miss Fiery Independence?"

Oh, yeah. That one.

She kept the smile on her face. He had just outright told her not to think that, just because he would undergo a day with the family, this was the next step in a developing relationship.

She had been an idiot to think anything like that could ever happen.

"Good," she said, acting as if none of it was chomping away at her heart. "We'll show them that there's no chance you're going to steal me away."

He agreed. "Yup, serves them right for being nosy enough to invite me over."

She laid her head on his shoulder, almost believing the fibs, too.

Sometime before Jackson awakened from sleep, he dreamed of red flags.

They had flown like warning banners that snapped in a brutal wind, surrounding him, whipping out at him, leaving welts on his arms.

Meet the family, he had heard in the wind. *Slip a ring on her finger, march up the aisle...*

Then, in his nightmare, those flags suddenly disappeared, leaving him standing in a void. But when he peered down at himself, he saw that he had been returned to normal—he was even back on his ranch now, in front of his cabin, wearing jeans and spurs on his boots while he carried a saddle.

He saw himself walking up the stairs to his door, and in a surreal haze, he knocked on it, as if he didn't even live there anymore.

The door opened, and all that emerged was

a hand, palm up, as if some kind of phantom was asking for something.

Inexplicably, Jackson knew just what it was, too, and he bent down, put his saddle on the porch and stripped off his spurs.

Somewhere, he heard the resurgent moan of the wind, as if it was saying, "Noooo."

He heard the snap of those red flags.

But he handed those spurs over, anyway, and, in return, those ghostly hands gave him a bunch of sharpened pencils.

At first, Jackson didn't know what was what—not until he looked down again to see that his jeans and boots had turned into a business suit and polished designer shoes.

A pencil-pushing geek…?

With a start, Jackson opened his eyes. Sweat cooled on his skin as his gaze found Laila sitting up next to him in bed, the covers bunched down around her waist, revealing the eyelet-flowered nightgown she was wearing. Her blond hair fell loose and wavy past her shoulders.

"Jackson?" she asked, touching his arm.

He glanced around, seeing that he was in Laila's cream-and-peach wallpapered bedroom, where nothing had changed.

And nothing would ever change.

Relieved, he ran a hand through his hair,

then sat up to give her a kiss good morning. But, just for good measure, he checked Laila's ring finger.

Nothing there.

"What're you doing?" she asked. "Are you okay?"

"Not really." He gave her another kiss, then pulled her onto his lap. "Just had a bad dream is all."

"Must've been a doozy."

"It was. But it's over."

She bit her lip, as if wondering if she should ask about the details. Or maybe she was even about to tell him that she'd had a bad dream, too.

Apparently, she decided against pursuing whatever it was, then ruffled his hair, scooting out of bed. His heart seemed to follow wherever she went.

He leaned back against his pillow, feeling as if this was the flip side of a dream—the good part.

But then he thought about those red flags again. Was he afraid that committing to Laila was going to make him into someone who would have to give up his thrilling playboy life for a much more sedate one?

Yeah. That was a pretty logical conclusion.

As they got ready for the morning—with her taking her usual jog to the market and him reading the paper as Lord Vader dillydallied in his fishbowl—Jackson wondered if he should still go to the Cates' ranch for Football Day.

After all, that dream had been his subconscious warning him off after yesterday, when her family had asked her to bring him over.

But Jackson thought of how Laila might feel if he stayed away. Strangely, he couldn't stand the notion of making her sad or embarrassing her, and that far outweighed any discomfort he might undergo.

Hell, he could handle the Cates family and come out of the experience unscathed.

When Laila came back from her jog/walk with chips and dip in her grocery bag, he was already showered and dressed. It didn't take her all that long to ready herself, too, and that shocked the sugar out of Jackson since he had always surmised that a beauty queen would take much longer than anyone else to primp.

Then again, if Laila had taught him anything, it was that she wasn't any normal Miss Fiery Independence.

They arrived at the Cates Ranch about a half hour before kickoff and, just before climbing out of the truck, Laila smoothed out her Bobcats sweatshirt and adjusted Jackson's shirt collar under his coat.

"When they inevitably grill you," she said, "I predict it'll be with finesse. You won't have to worry about my brother or dad—they'll no doubt be talking about the football. Besides, I'm sure they'll respect that Man Code you all have going. But my mom and sisters…?"

"Wait—Man Code?" he asked.

"Yeah. Where it's pretty much agreed that the women of the house will take care of all the jawdroppingly intrusive questions."

"How do you know this if you've never invited a guy over before?"

Laila smiled, and his eyes were drawn to that beauty spot near one upper corner of her lips. His stomach tumbled, the rest of him wishing he could get her out of here and alone for the rest of the day.

"Believe me," she said. "I know my family well enough to make guesses about their behavior. But don't worry—I'll run interference and deal with all the overexcited woman queries. And I'm sure they'll see early on that there's nothing serious happening, and they'll back away from the grilling and leave us alone within the first hour."

"Boy—you've got this all planned out, don't you?"

She kissed him on the cheek, then exited

the truck, leaving him wondering why he felt a little empty because of this plan of hers.

Was it because it felt...unreal?

He recalled that awful dream he'd had this morning and decided that he would go along with her scheme, unreal or not.

Mr. Cates met them at the front door, and from the first second, Jackson could tell by the way he looked at Laila that her prediction had been very wrong.

She was clearly the apple of his eye—even if he *had* wanted a son so desperately that he and his wife had birthed five daughters to get there.

If she had said that the men of the family would be a piece of cake to deal with, Jackson dreaded what was in store with the women.

"Dad!" Laila said as she hugged him.

Meanwhile, Zeke Cates kept eyeing Jackson over her shoulder.

Jackson merely put on the charm, hoping it would work with the big man.

Laila broke away from the embrace, gesturing to Jackson, but before she could introduce him, Zeke stuck out his hand for a shake.

"I know who Jackson Traub is," he said.

Jackson tried not to think that Zeke, like everyone else, had heard a thing or two about him around Thunder Canyon and was putting out a stern warning in the guise of a polite handshake.

When they gripped hands, Zeke's shake was enough to crush bones.

Yup, Father Bear had kept his ears open in town.

"Glad to meet you," Jackson said.

Laila laughed, then casually forced the two men's hands apart.

"Dad," she said.

Zeke took the hint from his daughter, then spread out his arm to welcome them into his home.

As Jackson and Laila entered, he could feel the older man's eyes still lasering into him.

"Sorry," Laila whispered.

They walked into a family room where Brody, the youngest of the Cates brood, greeted Jackson. He looked to be in his early twenties, and his welcome was hearty and easy enough to make Jackson semi-comfortable.

Then he heard a woman's voice from behind him.

"This must be Jackson."

Turning around, he found himself face-to-face with a beautiful woman who couldn't be anyone but Laila's mother.

She didn't settle for a handshake, going in for a hug straight off.

As Jackson responded in kind, he glanced at Laila, who was shooting him an impressed yet confused look. She apparently had misread both her mom and her dad. Hell, Zeke was even behind his wife, trying to seem as if he wasn't about to just take Jackson by the ear and drag him into the nearest private room for that grilling that was supposed to come from the Cates females.

Maybe the ladies in this family would be far stealthier in their social ways, Jackson thought. Laila had said there would be some female finesse involved.

Laila introduced him to her mom. "Evelyn Cates, Jackson Traub."

"Great to have you here." Evelyn was wearing a high ponytail, plus a frilly gingham apron swiped by flour over a pair of faded jeans.

"Thank you, ma'am."

"Oh, for heaven's sake—no ma'ams, please." Evelyn was undoing her apron and, judging by the heavy aroma of baked cake in the air, cooking time was done.

Jackson acknowledged her with a nod. He had taken off his hat, but now he shed his coat. Laila grabbed them, yet she didn't leave the room.

And that was probably because of what came next—a whole fleet of lovely women, every one of them smiling at Jackson as if they had a list of questions for him.

For the first time in his life, he didn't want to be in a room full of females.

With a stern expression—one that Jackson thought might serve to caution her sisters about getting fresh—Laila introduced him all around. He already knew some of their names, but, nevertheless, he could barely keep up with who was who. Maybe that was only because his mind was spinning, filled with the remnants of his psychotic dream from this morning. Any second, he expected one of the sisters to raise a red flag and another to hand him a bunch of pencils.

"Mom," Laila said, standing in front of her sisters as if she could keep them at bay, then handing Evelyn her bag of chips and dip. Her mom took his coat and hat, too. "Can we help you in the kitchen?"

The other woman got a sly smile on her face. "Yes—I think we do need some help."

As she urged Laila forward, she winked at Jackson. He hadn't realized it, but Brody had disappeared during all the fuss.

"Come along," Jazzy said, pushing at her siblings and laughing all the while.

The only Cates woman who remained a little behind was Abby, her long brown hair contrasting with all the blond in the room. She sent Jackson a long, considered glance, then turned around without comment.

All right then.

As they all entered the dining area, Jackson saw the reason that Brody had disappeared.

"Happy early birthday!" said Laila's brother as he held a pink-frosted cake with a bunch of lit candles.

Everyone else yelled it out, right before launching into a lively version of the birthday song, clapping along. The Cates family had a crazy way of singing it, though, just as Laila had indicated, with some kind of harmonizing that came off as goofy and endearing.

When they were done, they hugged Laila, kissing her, making her laugh.

But as Jackson took his turn in embracing her—and he made sure it was merely a friendly hug—he saw something in her eyes that he doubted anyone else had caught in all the gaiety.

Sadness? The reflection of thirty plus one-to-grow-on candles burning in her gaze…the specter of a future that she wasn't so certain about.

As her family celebrated around her, Jackson also realized that none of them really understood what this birthday meant to Laila.

His heart cracked a bit at that, and he rested a hand on her shoulder, letting her know that he, of all people, got it.

But it didn't seem to be enough. Not to him, anyway.

Sending a smile to him, Laila turned toward the cake, closed her eyes, made a silent wish. What it was, he had no idea.

He wasn't even sure he wanted to know.

She blew out the candles with the help of her sisters, and they all applauded as her mom took the cake to the table.

"Let's dig in," Brody said, rubbing his hands together and grabbing a plate just before he began to load it with food. "The game's gonna start soon."

As the family buzzed around Laila, she kept looking at that cake with its guttered candles, and in that moment, Jackson vowed to make this as painless a birthday as possible for her.

Monday, after work, Laila went straight home.

Jackson had asked if it was okay for him to come by before Dana and a few of her other friends arrived to pick her up for a low-key dinner that they had planned a while ago, long before Jackson had come to Thunder Canyon.

Funny how things changed, Laila thought as she locked up her car. Funny how, now, she only wanted to spend this night—the first one of her new decade—with *him,* even if they weren't a true "couple."

She could tell that, after yesterday, her family wasn't as sure as they had been that Laila had finally found a man to settle with. She and Jackson had persuaded them during the day that he was merely one of her casual suitors by being friendly yet a bit distant with each other.

Had he decided that she would want him to act that way?

Maybe it was for the best, though. Yes, her sisters—and even her dad—had tried their darnedest to juice information about Laila and Jackson's dating status out of them. But by the end of the first game, after she and Jackson had sat in separate chairs and kept their hands off each other, it was obvious that the brood had run out of questions for them, thinking that Laila was just being Laila and would lose interest in Jackson within a few weeks.

It was a relief, because that was what she and Jackson had been aiming for, right? And, even though Dad had eventually warmed up to

Jackson during the day and her sisters, Brody and Mom had clearly liked him, Laila had kept reminding them about how he wasn't intending to live in Thunder Canyon, for the long term.

That was the part that had put the lid on any more speculation from Laila's sisters—the part that had reemphasized that the relationship would go no further than a fling.

And that was the part that weighed on Laila every time she thought about it.

She got to her door, opened it, stepping inside to a semidark room, lit only by the hint of light from her kitchen.

"Jackson?"

Without a word, he walked into the family room and when she saw what he was holding, her chest constricted.

It was a lopsided cake with one burning candle on it.

The lone flicker lit the smile on his face. "Happy birthday, Laila."

She didn't trust herself to speak through the sudden, sharp tightness in her throat.

He set the cake on the end table by the sofa, near Lord Vader's bowl, then dug into his jeans pocket, producing a little wrapped box.

He seemed almost shy, the smile on his face

uncertain, as if, maybe, he had overstepped the boundaries they had set with each other.

After handing that box to her, he said, "It's nothing big."

"You shouldn't have gotten me anything."

Still, she tore off the wrapping to find a black velvet box. Inside, there was a silver bracelet with intricate whirling designs. Tiny rubies were embedded within it.

She recognized the work from a custom boutique in Old Town, and their items weren't cheap.

"Jackson…"

"It was pretty. It'll look great on you."

He didn't say any more than that and, after she slipped on the bracelet, she glanced back at the cake. A bittersweet pain pierced her. So sweet, so *thoughtful*. He had gone to some effort, and that was what mattered the most.

"One candle," he said. "That's all I put on the cake because this is the start of something new for you. The first year of the rest of your life. We should all be able to start over every so often."

His words had a hopeful ring to them. It wasn't that he merely understood all the reasons that she had gotten quiet when she had seen all those candles on the cake yesterday—

Jackson knew what it was like to want to start over, too.

She wished she didn't have to blow out the candle. Yesterday, when she had done it, it had been as if she had been extinguishing the birthday wish she had made—the fervent hope that he *would* stick around, and that she could be enough to make him want that.

"You made this for me?" she asked, the words catching in her throat.

"I tried." He chuckled. "Can't say my future lies in the direction of baking, though."

"It's…beautiful." She bit her lip, afraid that she might start to cry, because it *was* beautiful. More than she dared to let him know.

"I realize," he said, "that Dana and the girls are going to pick you up soon and you're probably going to be having more cake tonight, but I just wanted…"

She went to him, enveloping him in a grateful hug. He had known just what she needed on this birthday.

He wrapped his arms around her, too—so tight, so comfortably.

"I wish I could just stay here with you tonight," she said into his chest.

She thought she felt his arms tense, and she remembered the bad dream he'd had yesterday morning. She had been watching him sleep, and he had never known that she had seen the emotions crossing his face—the wary lines, then the panic.

A bad dream. She had been having them, too, with her literally strolling around Thunder Canyon, barefoot and pregnant.

But it had dawned on her that it wasn't such a nightmare.

He leaned down, his mouth against the top of her head. "Is that the wish you're going to make when you blow out the candle—that you want to stay here with me tonight?"

"No." She rested her cheek against his broad chest. "I won't be gone all that long, anyway, so why waste a wish?"

He pressed her to him, and they remained that way, until the candle started to burn lower, wax coming to roll down the side like little tears.

"Make your wish, Laila," he said.

When she did, it had nothing to do with staying with him tonight.

I wish I could find a way to ask him to stay forever, she thought, blowing out the candle.

Chapter 11

Should she ask Jackson to stay?

Or would it be better to ask him to go before everything got way more involved and so much worse?

There was only one person Laila could think to turn to after the night of her birthday: the one person who had comforted her after her first and only bad mark on a book report in grammar school. The one person who had stroked her hair and told her everything would be all right when she had been turned down by her first choice of college.

The next morning, before going into work, Laila sat across from Mom at the kitchen table in the Cates ranch house, her hands cupping a mug of hot jasmine tea. Dad was taking a ride around the spread, so he wouldn't be back for a while.

"Are you sure you're feeling all right?" Mom asked, stirring sugar into her own mug.

"Yes, I'm fine."

Mom had already commented on Laila's flushed cheeks and put her hand over her daughter's forehead, thinking that she was here because she was under the weather. Laila wanted to say she was only heartsick. And that she had never moaned and groaned to anyone about a man before as she was about to do.

How should she start?

Mom made it easy on her, blue eyes brimming with compassion. "Your being here today has nothing to do with having the flu or a cold. Am I right?"

Laila nodded, taking the first step. And, already, it felt a little better.

"I never thought this would happen to me," she said, her voice on the verge of breaking.

Mom scooted her wooden chair closer to Laila's, leaning over to catch her eye. "Oh, honey, none of us can control what happens to our hearts. If we could, we'd all be drones." She clasped Laila's hand. "When you allowed

Jackson to come over on Sunday, I knew something big was up, even if you were fighting to hide it tooth and nail."

"I didn't do such a good job of hiding, did I?"

"Neither did he."

Her mom wouldn't tease her like this, and at the observation, her spirits lifted.

Mom squeezed Laila's hand. "Why don't you tell me about it?"

There was something about talking to your mom that you couldn't get from chatting with a best friend, Laila thought. Wisdom, experience, a ruthless sense of protection, and she held to Mom's hand for all those qualities.

"I have no idea when I started feeling this way about him," she said.

"Jackson?"

"Of course, Mom."

"Then just say his name. Come out with it."

"Jackson." There, she had finally put his name out there for all the world to hear, starting with her mother.

Laila risked a glance at her, finding Mom smiling, looking so young, as if she had been transported back years and years into her own memories.

"Even though you and Jackson were trying

to seem casual with each other when he came over," she said, "there was no fooling anyone. I would see him slip you a look, and you slip him one right back. Your dad and I would do the same, way back when."

"You still do that now. Except…"

"Except what?"

Laila forged ahead, broaching the deep-seated reasons she was here.

"Except," she said, "when there were times I thought you wished life had gone a little differently."

Mom frowned.

"Surely you know what I mean," Laila said. "You've always told me to develop my life outside of men. 'Don't rely on anyone else to make you feel valued'—that's what you've always said to *all* of us. And I took that to heart because…"

Mom pushed back a strand of hair that had slipped down to block Laila's face. "Because why?"

All those times Laila had seen the longing on her mom's face while she looked at those college catalogues, all those veiled comments about traveling to places she had never gotten to visit came back to Laila.

"Sometimes I think that you got married before you were ready," she said.

"Oh, honey. Yes, I did get married in my flush of youth, but I think you've misinterpreted some of the lessons I've tried to teach you."

"Am I wrong in thinking that you regret not being able to pursue your studies? And that you never got to sow your wild oats and live all by yourself before raising a family?"

Mom's smile was patient. "I wouldn't trade my life with Zeke for anything. Same with you kids. Maybe I enjoy indulging in the whole 'road not taken' fantasy about what my life could've been, but if I had never married or had children when I did, I would be so incomplete, Laila." She gave her a lowered glance, emphasizing her next point. "I encouraged you to develop a career and an independent spirit because I saw in you, even from a very young age, that you had a real fire. I wanted you to think about all your options because you had so many, but I never meant to scare you off marriage. I feel terrible that I did."

"Don't, Mom."

As her mother sighed and then sipped her tea, Laila allowed everything to soak in. Her mom was right. Somewhere along the way—in high school? college?—she might have taken all Mom's advice too far. She had become comfortable with being single, with being in control of life by controlling the men in it. And whenever that control threatened to break, as with her quarterback or architect, she had called it off.

Then there was Jackson, who had thrown her for more of a loop than any of them, and ceding some of the control that she had treasured made her feel as if she was allowing herself to become weak—to give up everything she had worked so hard to earn in life, like her job, her individuality.

"When you got married," Laila asked, "did you ever feel as if you were becoming... Well, something other than yourself?"

"You mean, did I feel as if Zeke was infringing on my personality and I would never have that part of myself back? Maybe. But I would've never become the person I am today—a person I love—if it wasn't for Zeke. I wouldn't give back who I am now for the world."

Laila drank some of her tea, realized it had gone a bit cold.

"There's more to it all than that, isn't there?" Mom asked.

"Yes." She put down her mug. "It's just that, for the longest time, I thought I could have it all—a career, a social life, freedom—while having men in my life. But with Jackson, I'm so afraid that I'll have to give up some of that."

"And you still want it all."

"Yes, Mom, I do."

But could she have it?

Mom said, "Truthfully, I'm not sure you can have it all—not at the same time. But I think you can find a balance as well as a lot of happiness in the effort."

Laila turned that over in her mind, but in her heart…

Her heart had already decided, and that was the reason she felt ripped apart between two warring factions. She had spent too much time being stridently single to give up everything she thought was at stake this easily.

Mom said, "Are *you* in love with Jackson?"

Even after all this, she was still too afraid to say it out loud.

Was she waiting until he said it first?

"Ah, well," Mom said, crossing one leg over the other as she got ready to sip from her mug again. "You don't have to tell me. A mother can always see into her child's heart."

"Like a crystal ball," Laila said, trying to smile.

"Just like that."

As Mom drank, Laila wondered if her mother was right—if she could see a future in which her daughter lived happily ever after with Jackson, with no regrets.

And no heartbreak from the Texas bad boy.

Even a couple of days later, Laila and Jackson were still doing their lying low routine, visiting each other's homes, spending the nights in each other's arms, going about their business as if nothing was threatening to break under the growing weight between them.

Laila would watch him when she believed he wasn't looking. Over dinner, on the sofa, she would silently will him to give her a sign that she could pour her soul out to him. There had been so many times when she had almost started up *the* conversation, but she had always chickened out.

Her need to tell him everything was pushing at her, though, and she didn't know how much longer she could last by staying silent.

There were even times when she told herself that maybe this was never meant to be, and she should just let it go. Getting over him would be easy once he was gone.

Today, she was with Dana during their lunch hour, shopping in a crafts boutique in

Old Town for spangles that her friend wanted to use on her "Liberty Belle" Halloween costume. Laila was just as distracted as she had been the past couple of days, if not more.

They were on the boardwalk, where other lunchtimers passed them.

"Earth to Laila," Dana said, bopping her with the craft store shopping bag.

Laila sent a vague smile to her friend. Then she realized that Dana wasn't going to let the subject go this time.

"Ever since your birthday," Dana said, "you've been off in the clouds."

"I'm here."

Her friend chuffed. "I see your body, but the inner Laila is AWOL."

Laila had spent so much time trying to sort this out herself that it was obvious she had gone into some kind of shell. It wasn't fair to any of her friends.

She glanced around, grabbed the sleeve of Dana's conservative bank jacket, then pulled her off the boardwalk. Others strolled by, watching, then moving on.

"I've been trying to do it," Laila said.

"Do…what?"

Her heart popped in her chest. "Tell Jackson that I'm ready."

No other explanation was required for Dana.

"You?" her friend asked, taking the Clark Kent glasses from their resting place on top of her head and putting them over her eyes, as if she couldn't see straight without them.

But Laila knew better. Those glasses were just for show in the bank.

"Yes, me," she said.

Dana enfolded Laila in a big hug, squeezing her hard. When she pulled back, she cuffed at a little wet streak that had leaked from her eye.

"Don't mind me," Dana said.

Laila held her hand. "I'm not going to leave you behind. And there isn't even a guarantee that Jackson—"

"Oh, of course he adores you." Dana fluttered a dramatic hand in front of her face. "It's obvious to everyone in town that the man would swim an ocean for you, but you're both such stubborn mules about admitting it." She sucked in a wobbly breath. "I'm so happy for you."

Laila hugged her again, and from the way Dana held to her, she knew this was about more than Laila deserting her. Dana and she had gone to their first school dance together, as fluttery as new butterflies as they had waited for a boy to cross the room and talk to them.

She and Dana had kept scrapbooks of their dreams and hopes.

She *was* happy for Laila.

They separated, both laughing, recovering, drawing more attention from everyone around them, but Laila didn't care. She was a new woman after admitting this to Dana—she felt as if she could go tell Jackson right now.

But she kept thinking that even a little pause from him, a hint that he wasn't going to commit right back to her, would shatter her.

So when would be the perfect time to let him know?

Dana linked arms with Laila as they stepped back onto the boardwalk. The day had a slight chill to it, and each of them pulled her jacket and coat tighter around them.

"Promise me," Dana said, "that you're not going to go all Bridezilla now."

"I promise." And she meant it. After all, Mom said there could be a balance, and Laila was going to find it.

As they strolled in the direction of a town square lunch cart to pick up something to take back to the bank, they passed the brick building where Traub Oil had its offices. Feeling a magnetic draw to it, Laila slowed her steps.

Dana pinched her. "There's still time on

lunch break to say hi to your boyfriend. Maybe even to tell him—"

Anxiety shook up Laila.

"Go!" Dana gave her a tiny push and then was on her way.

But Laila just stood there for a moment longer. Would Jackson see it on her face—that she had decided once and for all that he was the one for her?

A niggle haunted her. What if he had already seen it before and he had chosen not to do a damn thing about it?

She heard footsteps on the gravel behind her, and she turned to discover a mustached ranch hand in a low-riding cowboy hat, a thick flannel coat, a big silver belt buckle.

Duncan Brooks.

She sent him a polite smile as he awkwardly greeted her with a nod, his hands in his jeans pockets.

"Laila," he said.

He barely made eye contact with her, and she felt sorry for him in a way. He was a bit of a loner, and whenever she had talked with him before, it had been a stilted experience.

"Hello, Duncan," she said, spying his red-and-white pickup parked near the boardwalk. There were feedbags in the back of it, and she surmised that he must have made a store run here in town.

He didn't go anywhere, as if he was trying to figure out how to talk to her. Laila didn't want to be rude, so she waited him out.

Finally, he adjusted his hat, glancing up at the Traub Oil building.

"I don't want to presume, but I was just wonderin'… About that Halloween party your parents put on every year… You'll be attending that tomorrow night, won't you?"

She held up her bag from the crafts store. "I'm putting the finishing touches on my costume when I get home." She had been keeping her Snow Queen outfit a secret from Jackson, and he had, in return, teased her about the costume *he* was putting together. She doubted he would come as anything other than what he was.

A halo of warmth surrounded her heart.

And it all felt nice and wonderful until Duncan cleared his throat, then said, "I was only wondering… If you would… If you needed…"

Was he trying to ask her to the party?

"Duncan," she said gently, "I'm going with Jackson Traub. But we'll see you there, right?"

"Sure." He had gone tense, reminding her of Cade Pritchett after she had rejected him, too. She wished these situations didn't have to come up.

He started to tip his hat to her but hesitated.

Laila waited for him once more, hoping that he wasn't going to ask her out for a different time.

What he actually said startled her.

"Excuse my bluntness, Laila, but I can't believe you're with Jackson Traub. He doesn't respect you as you should be respected."

She shook her head, ready to argue. Duncan didn't know the real Jackson.

"He's going to use you and throw you away," Duncan said. "Mark my words."

"Why would you say that to me?"

Duncan shuffled in his boots, but when he spoke again, it was with some conviction. "He ain't keeping it a secret. I heard him not so long ago in the Rock Creek Diner, crowing to his cousin about how he only went after you because you're a pretty face. And when he goes away, he's going to do it without another thought."

Her legs felt brittle.

Just a pretty face...

Jackson couldn't have said that, much less in public, where someone like Duncan Brooks could overhear. Jackson knew how much it would wound her, because she had spilled out her soul to him about what it felt like to have people underestimate her. He had even told her to go out there and kick butt.

He had cared. He had changed from that bad boy who probably *would* have run around town being so callous.

Hadn't he?

Duncan saw her doubt, and he took off his hat and held it over his heart. "I'm so sorry, Laila. I just thought it was fair to let you know."

He gave her one last sympathetic glance before putting his hat back on and walking away toward his pickup.

Numb, Laila didn't move. The man who had charmed her, snuck his way into her heart, where no one had ever been before…

According to Duncan, that man had said *that* about her.

She still couldn't believe it, because if he *had* said it, it would mean that, all this time, he had only taken what he wanted from her, setting her up for the big fall when, after he left, he wouldn't have to stick around to pick up the pieces. He had been every bad thing anyone had ever said about him.

Worse yet, had Jackson really *ever* seen anything in her but her looks?

As the numbness went from her chest all through her body, she had to wonder if she would ever be more to anyone than a Barbie doll.

A trophy that a bad boy would grab and leave behind when the shininess wore off.

Chest tight, hardly able to breathe, she looked at the brick Traub Oil building, but the stinging blur of her gaze made it hard to see much more than a big, slashed red heart.

Jackson had been standing by his tinted office window for about ten minutes now as he talked on the speakerphone with his twin, Jason, who had called him just to catch up.

But it was hard to concentrate on a phone call when he could see Laila down below, near the oak-laced town square. She and Dana were down there, and he wondered if Laila was going to come into the building.

In anticipation, his pulse twirled, imitating the swirly candle he had put on her birthday cake the other night.

Just remembering how it had felt to see her so happy at a simple gesture—one he had made so easily—swept him away again.

If one smile from her could make his night, what could she do to the rest of his life?

God help him, but he wanted to know. He just had to find the right time to put his heart out there, to take the risk of telling her.

But would she decide that they had no future and turn him down, just as she had done to her former boyfriends who had come close, only to leave with their hearts on the floor?

Jackson almost forgot he was on the phone with Jason.

"Hey," said his brother from over the line. "Where did you go?"

Jackson turned away from the window. "I'm here."

Even though he couldn't see Laila any more, it was as if he still had her in his sights, vivid, everpresent.

"So what about Thanksgiving?" Jason asked. "Mom wants to know if you can make it down."

"I…" What was Laila doing for Thanksgiving?

His office door opened, and Ethan and Corey entered, both taking quiet scats in the leather chairs under the lasso clock on the wall.

"Damn, Jackson," Jason said. "Maybe I'll just call back."

Ethan spoke up. "He's only in La-La Land, Jace. Give him a break."

"His brain is mush," Corey said, "because he's got a real live *girlfriend.*"

He drew that last word out, and Jackson leaned over to his desk, grabbed a piece of paper, wadded it up and then threw it at both his brothers. It hit Corey in the head and ricocheted over to Ethan, winging his shoulder.

Both brothers thought that was hilarious, and Jackson went for another piece of paper.

"What the hell is going on there?" Jason asked. "Are you running a madhouse?"

"Pretty much," Ethan said, ducking Jackson's follow-up.

"Next time," Jackson said to Ethan and Corey, "it'll be the pencil holder coming at you."

They pretended to be scared, then laughed, stretching out their legs, getting cozy.

Unable to help himself, Jackson wandered back to the window, just to catch a glimpse of Laila again.

When he saw she was now talking to that cowpoke, Duncan Brooks, he remained at the window, yet another unfamiliar emotion claiming him.

Jealousy.

Jason said, "Jackson, when you decide about Thanksgiving, give Mom a call. She's waiting, and you know she doesn't like to be kept on a hook."

"I'll do that."

His twin hung up, but Ethan and Corey didn't make a move to leave. Jackson wasn't even paying much attention to them because his full focus was on Laila, who had gone from a polite posture with Duncan Brooks to tilting her head, leaning forward a little, as if she was trying to understand something he was telling her. His hat was even over his heart.

What the hell?

Corey said, "Why don't you bring Laila to Thanksgiving, Jackson? Mom and Pete would love to meet her."

"I think it's time," Ethan said.

Yeah, Jackson thought. Time for him to walk downstairs and see what was going on.

He went for the door, still seeing Duncan with his cowboy hat in that heart-covering position, as if he was calling on Laila for a dance or something.

After going down the stairs, he came to the lobby, just as Laila entered the doors.

He didn't ask what she had been talking about with Duncan Brooks. Hell, no—she had a fire in her eyes that told Jackson something bad had happened out there.

"Tell me it's not true," she said, her voice sounding as if it had been shredded.

And…the hurt. It was all over her for some reason—from her tortured expression to her fisted hands.

"Laila?" he asked.

She headed for the side of the lobby as people looked after her. Jackson ignored them and followed her, straight to the women's restroom, where the door had just been shut.

Knocking, he repeated, "Laila?"

Without waiting for an answer, he eased open the door, hoping no one else besides Laila was in there.

And it was empty, but for her. She had her hands braced on the counter, her head down, leaving a long strand of hair that had escaped from her barrette covering her face.

"Did I do something?" he asked, shutting the door behind him.

When she glanced up at him, her gaze was reddened, as if she was about to cry.

"What did Duncan Brooks say to you?" Jackson asked, ready to go after him.

"He…"

When Jackson went over to her, she backed away toward the wall.

The breath bolted out of Jackson. He recovered just enough to say, "I don't understand..."

She merely shook her head, and it seemed as if she had to gather everything she had within her just so she could speak.

"Once, I asked you if you had set your cap for the local beauty queen when you came here."

The suspicion about what Duncan Brooks had told Laila crept over Jackson with the slow surety of coming devastation.

"I asked you," she continued, "if the only reason you invited me out was because you wanted to add me to your collection. You said no." Her expression crumbled. "Now that I think about it, you didn't even deny it. You went on to tell me that, when you first saw me, you noticed a spark, and that's why you wanted to get to know me."

"I did," he said, knowing now that it had been so much more than just a spark.

She shook her head, her eyes even mistier now. "Duncan Brooks heard you say something that puts you in a whole other category than who I thought you were."

His world started to wobble. Why hadn't he just told her earlier that he hadn't meant to say what he had said? That, at the time, he had wanted to take it back, even though he had desperately been trying to persuade himself that he wasn't falling for her?

"I should've told you all about that conversation I had with DJ in the diner," he said.

She went back to the counter, leaning against it as if her faith in him had been the only thing holding her up until now.

He continued, hoping that he could redeem himself. "It was wrong of me, Laila. And I didn't mean a word of it. If I could take it back, I surely would, but—"

"Do you know how it makes me feel to know that you're just like the rest of them?" she whispered.

Like the rest of them—adoring her for her beauty, never bothering to look any deeper.

It was like a bladed thrust to everything he had started to believe about himself since he had met her. But she didn't give him the opportunity to tell her that he had changed, and it was because of her.

His love for her.

She wiped at her eyes, struggling like hell to overcome more tears, and her fight to do so ripped at him.

"You really are a playboy," she said. "I just bought into your act."

Now he was the one who needed the crutch of the counter, although he kept himself from reaching out for it.

Laila, the only one who had seemed to look past *his* reputation. He had pushed her too far.

"Laila," he said, "the only reason I said what I said to DJ is that I didn't know what else to do. I…"

The words—the big *I've-fallen-for-you* ones—almost escaped from his mouth, but then instinct took over, years and years of self-preservation.

Besides, she wasn't going to believe that he had changed. He had already done enough damage to her that she would remember this moment—this heart-killing crash—every time she saw him from now on.

As she rushed out of the room, the door slammed behind her, just as she had shut the door on him before, on their first date when he had teased her to the point of frustration.

It seemed like a lifetime ago.

He turned, looked in the mirror at Jackson Traub, seeing the pain in his eyes.

Seeing a crushed man who was missing something vital without Laila.

Chapter 12

That night, Jackson sat at the dining table in his condo, a beer in hand, trying to drown his sorrows.

But he had no taste for it any more.

None of it.

He had left the office early, intent on going out, chasing a good time and forgetting about Laila altogether...

Unfortunately, even *that* had left a taste as bad as this beer.

Now, with every swallow, he realized that he didn't want to forget the feel of her silky blond hair tangled through his fingers, her smooth skin under his hands, her soft mouth—the softest and most desirable in the world—murmuring sweet nothings under his kisses…

Jackson thumped the bottle onto the table. This wasn't working at all. Hell, he hadn't even gotten through one beer yet and he already felt hung over.

How could he cure himself, though?

Not for the first time, he was tempted to grab his phone, call her, apologize. But he knew it wouldn't be enough. And he knew that if he showed up at her doorstep full of more excuses, it wouldn't do any good, either.

He tugged a hand through his hair just as a knock sounded on his door. When he didn't answer, his phone rang.

Checking the ID screen, he saw DJ's name. Crap.

Instead of answering his cell, Jackson went to the door and pulled it open. DJ was on the other side, closing his own phone, making Jackson's generic ringtone come to a halt.

His cousin took one look at Jackson and said, "They told me you were a disaster when you left. They were being kind."

When Jackson had last seen his brothers, it had been post-Laila, after he had numbly climbed the stairs and gone to his office, sat in his chair for a while just staring straight ahead of him, then left. Corey and Ethan had tried to talk to him, asking him what had happened, but Jackson hadn't responded.

He hadn't had the heart.

Without being invited in, DJ brushed past Jackson, shedding his coat and hanging it on the rack.

"What're you doing?" Jackson asked.

DJ went to the living area and took a seat on a stuffed leather couch. "Babysitting you. Your brothers seem to think that you're going to get into some trouble tonight."

"Why aren't they here to stop me?"

Raising an eyebrow, DJ said, "Let's think back to a few months ago… Corey's wedding…? Fists flying, Traub brothers brawling, you leading the way…?"

Jackson just wiped a hand over his face, then sat on the opposite end of the couch from DJ. "And that's why they sent you—because you're the most diplomatic of the family."

"They know that something's really wrong, Jackson, and they're ready to swing over here at a moment's notice if you need them."

In spite of that assurance, Jackson felt more isolated than ever. He loved his brothers, but they weren't Laila.

He had allowed her glimpses that no one else had gotten—or he feared would *ever* get.

"Word is," DJ said, his brown eyes full of sympathy, "Laila ran crying out of the Traub Oil building just before you came upstairs. Why?"

No hiding it anymore.

But Jackson didn't even *want* to hide it. He just wanted her here again.

He broke down, telling DJ just about everything: the flirtation that he thought wouldn't ever get so serious, the part where they had *gotten* more serious, the seriousness of what he was feeling now.

"What I told you at the Rock Creek Diner… When I said that I had wooed Laila just because she was beautiful…?" Jackson shook his head. "I was wrong. Even then, I was attracted to her for a whole other reason, but I didn't have an inkling of what it was."

"Now you know it was love."

See—even DJ knew it.

Jackson leaned his forearms on his thighs. "Now I don't even want to drive a mile out of Thunder Canyon because it'd be too far from her. I couldn't admit that back then or today, though. And when Laila confronted me with what I said, I should've…"

Revealed his heart to her.

Should've, could've, would've…

"Jeez, Jackson," DJ said. "It's obvious that you're a mess, and if you don't go to her and tell her everything, you're never going to forgive yourself. Believe me."

"Is that what you did with Allaire?"

DJ's face took on a glow, one that Jackson had also felt when he had been watching Laila from his office window today, moments before she had come into the building and dismantled his life.

"My wife," DJ said, "was the one who didn't know what she wanted. I always did, even when we were younger. Allaire just needed a big gesture from me—needed to see that I was never going to give up, no matter how tough the going got."

And, suddenly, every bleary thing around Jackson got a little clearer.

"If Laila's what you really want," DJ said, "then humbling yourself is a strong first step, Jackson. You've got to show her that this obstacle is nothing compared to how you feel about her. That is, if you're ready."

Jackson remembered that man in the mirror—the distraught "disaster" who had lost his heart when Laila had run out of the restroom.

And it was just a matter of getting up off this couch and getting his tail in gear to show Laila that he *had* become a better man because of her.

"I'm ready," Jackson said.

As DJ stood by, the first thing Jackson did was suck up his courage, calling Mrs. Cates to explain, apologize...

...and hopefully to plan.

The next evening at the Cates ranch house, Zeke and Evelyn's annual Halloween bash was in full swing.

Every costume from that of a joker to a witch to a ghost was represented by the guests. The house was decorated with Halloween streamers and doodads: Crones on broomsticks hanging from the ceiling, huge sparkling spiderwebs in corners, paper skeletons dangling on the walls. The aromas of pumpkin cake and caramel-dipped apples filled the air while howling, haunted house sounds added to the festive atmosphere.

Laila was standing near her mom's upright piano, which was shrouded with cobwebs, in the family room with Dana. Her friend, outfitted as a red-white-and-blue-spangled Statue of Liberty, had decorated herself with a couple of flourishes to make her the belle of the ball: her hair was streaked with patriotic colors, her toga swirling with firecracker designs, her Victorian ankle boots decorated with ribbons.

Even though Laila had thought about not coming to the party altogether, much less wearing the long ethereal white dress with snowflake sparkles that made up much of her Snow Queen costume, Dana had dragged her out of the apartment. Laila had gone along with it only because she knew that her family would never let her live it down if she begged out of the party. Mom, in particular, had put the hard sell on Laila to attend last night. Even when Laila had countered that things weren't going so well with Jackson and she would rather stay home, her mom had told her that what she truly needed was to be here.

"Trust me," Mom had said.

So here Laila was, and the more she saw people having fun around her, the more she asked herself why she was allowing a relationship that was only supposed to be brief in the first place to get her down.

She would be darned if she let anyone see how much agony she was experiencing because of Jackson.

"Another glass of punch?" Dana asked,

keeping her eye on some single men from town who had been invited by Laila's parents. They were trading jokes with Matt and Marlon, Laila's cousins, plus their fiancées, Haley Anderson and Elise Clifton.

"I'm punched out," Laila said.

She sure *felt* that way, too, as if she had been blindsided after a slam to the stomach. Last night, she had left work early and ghostwalked through the rest of the day. It had only been when she had lain down in her empty bed that she had figuratively hit the floor, knocked out.

Obviously, Jackson hadn't cared enough to call her after their fight. Maybe she had shamed him into believing that she thought he was dirt.

What man would come around after that?

But, damn her, with every beat of her heart, that was all she wanted him to do—reach out and explain.

Unless…

She tried not to think about it, but the mental specter was always there…

Unless he truly *had* been using her for a disposable good time. Unless she genuinely was just a crown that he could claim and brag about.

But, if that was the case, what about the way

he had kissed her? What about the way he had looked at her as he had held her in his arms?

Heart heavy, Laila toyed with a spiderweb on the piano until Dana cleared her throat.

"Just hang in there," her friend said way more optimistically than Laila could understand. "You'll be okay. Trust me."

Her mom had said the same thing.

Laila nodded, and Dana gave her a one-armed hug. A diamondlike snowflake sparkle floated out of Laila's unbound hair, where she had pinned a bunch of them.

Laila watched the glittering flake drift to the ground then sit on the carpet, as lifeless as she felt. And just as useless.

Someone was laughing nearby, and when Laila glanced up, she saw that Jazzy had brought Annabel and Jordyn over to Marlon and Matt, plus the pack of construction workers who had wandered over with water guns and green face paint slashed over their cheekbones. Army men, on the go. Nearby, Abby hung out with Brody, every once in a while casting a compassionate glance Laila's way.

Dammit, she felt like the poor loser among the bunch.

She smiled at Abby, showing that she could be just as good without Jackson.

Abby toasted her with her punch glass.

"Well," Dana said, glancing at her bicentennial watch as if she was expecting someone, though Laila couldn't imagine who. "I've got to powder my nose. You?"

Laila told herself that the pain in her chest would go away in a minute. "No, I'm fine."

"It's okay for girls to trek to the restroom together, you know. It's not a party foul."

"Really, you don't have to handle me with kid gloves." Now she felt like she was baggage.

Would she ever feel normal again?

She doubted it, because it seemed as if her ribs had been pried open and her heart excised. A macabre Halloween prank come early.

Maybe she should've dressed up as an unfeeling ghoul.

Dana touched Laila's arm, said she would be right back, then made her way through the crowd toward the hallway.

Laila was just about to force herself to join most of her sisters—who were dressed alike as Greek muses—when someone new walked into the room.

It was Dean Pritchett, and he was with his brother Nick, neither of whom had dressed up as more than Western outlaws with fake guns and holsters by their sides.

Was it Laila's imagination, or did Abby perk up a little on her side of the room?

Just as Laila thought she might have, her little sister seemed to lose interest in the Pritchett brothers.

Something told Laila that it was because Cade wasn't with them, but she shushed that thought away. Abby had explained about her friendship with Cade, and it was ridiculous to doubt her.

Dean spotted Laila and came over while Nick joined her other sisters, hugging Jazzy, Jordyn then Annabel hello.

Greeting Laila with a friendly embrace, Dean started up some small talk before he broke the *real* ice and said, "Cade is working overtime on a project, so he won't be around for a while tonight."

She knew how Cade got with his woodworking, but she also wondered if he had stayed away from the party because he thought she would be here with Jackson.

What a tangled web.

Dean spotted her parents and waved them over to say hi. Dad was dressed as Buffalo Bill Cody, fake beard and all, and Mom was Annie Oakley. And if all of them were attempting to entertain Laila and put Jackson out of her mind by being extra lively and talkative, it almost worked.

Almost, because in her chest, she could still feel that injury he had left—the soreness around her heart.

Why *couldn't* she give him one more chance to tell her who he might be now instead of who he had been a few weeks ago? Didn't she owe herself at least that? Some closure?

All Laila could hear were moaning creaks and cackles from the haunted house sound track.

She must have looked pretty pathetic standing there alone in the crowd, because Mike Trudeau even came over to talk to her. He was dressed as a huntsman and actually hadn't even been around the bank all week, due to another trip to the woods.

"Evening, Laila," her boss said.

"Hi, Mike."

He tapped his fingers against his punch glass, apparently trying to whip up the courage to say something to her.

He finally found it. "Being out of town this week, I'm afraid I didn't get around to apologizing for something that requires it. Maybe Jackson already told you, but…"

Jackson…

"I'm not sure what you're talking about," Laila said, although she suspected this had something to do with the chat Mike and Jackson had been having at the town hall, when it seemed as if Jackson wasn't too happy with her boss.

"He *didn't* tell you?" he said.

"No…"

Her words disappeared. She hadn't asked Jackson what he had been talking about with Mike Trudeau. Hadn't wanted to know because it went against all the "fling" and "temporary" markers that they had forced on themselves.

Her boss pursed his lips, then came out with it. "I haven't been entirely fair to you in work matters, Laila, and Jackson pointed that out to me. He about tore my head off, as a matter of fact." He nodded. "You deserve to have someone like him around, taking up your back as he does. Frankly, I'm surprised that he didn't crow to you about how he came to your rescue."

…*taking up your back like he does*…

Her boss motioned toward the entryway. "It's just that I thought I should get in my apologies to you before he came inside the house to make sure that I—"

She had already put her punch glass down on the piano, going toward the door.

"Laila?" called Dana from somewhere inside the party.

She smacked into a wall of man, gasped, looking up into the one face she had been aching to see.

An implosion rocked her. He hadn't dressed in costume—he was who he was in a long-sleeved Western shirt, jeans and boots. His hair was tousled from having taken off his hat, and, in one hand, he was holding a bunch of long-stemmed red roses.

They locked gazes for a moment that was battered by the anguish of yesterday. But there was something else in it, too.

As Laila stood away from him, her hand to her chest, her heart raced, as if it wanted to take off.

Or push her back into his arms.

"Evelyn," said Jackson. Her mom had come up behind them. "Thank you for extending the invitation."

Invitation?

As Mom stood beside Jackson, she gave Laila an innocent look, then grabbed onto Dad's hand as he arrived, too. He seemed on guard, although Laila knew he had taken a gruff shine to Jackson by the end of Football Day. It was clear, though, that Mom had explained to him what was going on right now, and he was behind whatever plans she had concocted.

Had Jackson gotten together with Mom to broker a truce and now everyone was in on this?

Laila thought of how Dana had made sure she had gotten here, no excuses tolerated, and how her siblings had welcomed her with overly open arms.

Her brother, sisters and Dana formed a circle around Jackson and Laila, as if waiting for something big to happen.

He said, "Don't be angry with your Mom, Laila. I told her what happened, and when she heard me out, she asked me to come over. I'm glad the whole family is here, too, because I have something real important to say, and it starts with a heartfelt apology about everything I've done in the past."

The Halloween special effect noises kept on, a whistling wind that added to the tension. Besides that, Laila heard someone mutter in the background.

"Here he goes, making another scene."

Jackson heard it, and he obviously knew what the peanut gallery was referring to.

"This isn't my brother Corey's wedding," he said in a level voice. "I haven't had any champagne tonight, and I'm not going to be making any speeches about how marriage stinks and how the entire state of matrimony is a big mistake. That's not why I'm here."

Someone else coughed, as if they doubted Jackson. Maybe they had been at the wedding and they couldn't imagine that there was any difference in him between then and now.

But he *had* grown up, becoming a man Laila could not only desire, but love. That was why yesterday had hurt so much, because of the suspicion that she had been wrong.

Yet, now, he waited before her, braving her family and friends, not knowing how she would react to him, standing tall with all those apology roses in hand.

A burn crept up her throat, her eyes stinging as Jackson stepped forward, handing her the flowers. Every petal seemed to tell her how much she was worth to him. If she couldn't read it in the bouquet, she sure could do it from the look in his eyes.

He was making a big gesture but, truly, all she had needed was him.

Jackson's pulse was racing a mile a minute as he stood there holding those roses. He felt every eye in the room on him, especially those of Laila's family.

Do her wrong again, they seemed to be saying, *and there'll be a high cost.*

But he was here to do right.

This time when he proposed, it was for real—not some joke at a beauty pageant.

"Laila, it wasn't so long ago that I didn't deserve to tread in the footsteps you made. But somewhere along the line, you brought a light to my head. And to my heart. You showed me decency, patience…even sweetness." He could barely breathe. "I can't see a future without you, and I ask with humility, hope and—Lord believe it—seriousness for you to spend the rest of your days with me."

The Halloween noises over the stereo abruptly stopped as a kind soul turned off the sound track. That left the high volume of Jackson's heartbeat in his ears as Laila broke into tears.

The flowers seemed to wilt in his arms.

Crying?

Was that how a woman said yes?

But then, just as he was at his lowest, she rushed to him, and he dropped the roses so he could pull her against him full force.

"I do," she whispered into his ear. "I will.

We will. My boss just told me what you said to defend me at the town hall. I wanted so badly to believe in you, though, even before he—"

"It's okay, Laila. Just so you say yes tonight."

The entire room broke into cheers and applause, but they were only wisps of noise while Jackson cupped Laila's head with one hand, her back with the other, holding on for dear life.

Then she raised her tear-stained face to him, and he realized that he still had so much to tell her, so much to straighten out.

But when she kissed him, he knew that everything would work. No doubts in his head, heart, soul.

They escaped out the door, but not before she grabbed their coats from the entry. She pulled him out front, where dusk was just lying down for the night and the lights from the ranch house windows breathed softly, like warm relief.

When she put on her coat, her flowing white dress whisked out from her hem. The last of the sunlight caught the diamond snowflake glitters in her long hair.

A queen, he thought. His queen for the rest of his life.

Then he remembered.

"Dammit," he said, stopping their progress. "I clean forgot."

As she faced him, he reached into his jeans pocket, coming out with a diamond ring that matched her sparkle. He had bought it today, mulling over the jewelry counter in Bozeman with care and consideration. With the hope that she wouldn't turn him down.

When she saw it, she sucked in a breath.

"I bought it," he said, "after giving a lot of thought to how I was going to go about winning you back. And I've been doing a lot of that during our relationship, haven't I? Always trying to woo, to win."

"That's because I demand effort," she said, nestling close to him, stroking his cheek with her fingertips. "Maybe too much at times."

"You were doing what I needed you to do, Laila. And, yesterday, when you came to me, all teared up…"

"No more apologies."

But he wanted there to be no trace of doubt, and he framed her face with his hands, looking down into those soul-deep blue eyes.

"I take a while to learn. And, for most of my life, I've been real comfortable not learning, just staying in a rut, marching to the same love-'em-and-leave-'em tune. I thought that I truly believed that a one-woman existence wasn't for me. I'd seen what love did to my mom after Dad's death, and *I* knew what it felt like to lose him, too. I never wanted to feel that way again."

"I know, Jackson."

He peered down at her. "You had me figured out long before I even did?"

"There was a lot to untangle, but I saw through you pretty early on, just as you did with me."

They were the only two people who could do that for each other, Jackson thought. Maybe that talent was a big part of love, and since he had never found it before, he'd had no idea when it had hit him so swiftly and thoroughly.

She laughed through her tears, and he dried them with the pad of his thumb, not liking to see her cry, wanting to do anything he could to stop it from this day forward.

"It was such a stupid fight," she said. "Wasn't it?"

"I was the cause of it. It was bound to come, anyway, with all we weren't saying to each other. I'm just glad we're on the same page now."

"The page that says we've also figured out our future plans?"

She was asking if he wanted to go back to Texas, abandoning Thunder Canyon.

But this town had caught his fancy, too, and he knew that staying here was important to Laila.

"Thunder Canyon is my home now," he said, "just as much as you are."

He took her hand in his, looking at her as if she were the diamond-studded heavens all wrapped into one woman.

Slipping the ring over her finger, he said, "My wife-to-be."

She looked at the ring for thc longest time, and he realized that she was crying again.

But when they connected gazes, he saw that they were good tears, and that made him happier than he ever thought he could be.

"My husband," she said, and he liked the sound of that.

Liked it way more than a former scoundrel like Jackson Traub would have ever thought.

Lost and found in each other, they kissed under the setting sun, the two least likely people to ever find love finally discovering it with each other.

* * * * *

Get 4 FREE REWARDS!

We'll send you 2 FREE Books plus 2 FREE Mystery Gifts.

FREE
Value Over
$20

Both the **Harlequin®** Special Edition and **Harlequin®** Heartwarming™ series feature compelling novels filled with stories of love and strength where the bonds of friendship, family and community unite.

YES! Please send me 2 FREE novels from the Harlequin Special Edition or Harlequin Heartwarming series and my 2 FREE gifts (gifts are worth about $10 retail). After receiving them, if I don't wish to receive any more books, I can return the shipping statement marked "cancel." If I don't cancel, I will receive 6 brand-new Harlequin Special Edition books every month and be billed just $5.24 each in the U.S. or $5.99 each in Canada, a savings of at least 13% off the cover price or 4 brand-new Harlequin Heartwarming Larger-Print books every month and be billed just $5.99 each in the U.S. or $6.49 each in Canada, a savings of at least 20% off the cover price. It's quite a bargain! Shipping and handling is just 50¢ per book in the U.S. and $1.25 per book in Canada.* I understand that accepting the 2 free books and gifts places me under no obligation to buy anything. I can always return a shipment and cancel at any time by calling the number below. The free books and gifts are mine to keep no matter what I decide.

Choose one: ☐ **Harlequin Special Edition**
(235/335 HDN GRCQ)
☐ **Harlequin Heartwarming Larger-Print**
(161/361 HDN GRC3)

Name (please print)

Address   Apt #

City   State/Province   Zip/Postal Code

Email: Please check this box ☐ if you would like to receive newsletters and promotional emails from Harlequin Enterprises ULC and its affiliates. You can unsubscribe anytime.

Mail to the **Harlequin Reader Service:**
IN U.S.A.: P.O. Box 1341, Buffalo, NY 14240-8531
IN CANADA: P.O. Box 603, Fort Erie, Ontario L2A 5X3

Want to try 2 free books from another series! Call 1-800-873-8635 or visit www.ReaderService.com.

---

*Terms and prices subject to change without notice. Prices do not include sales taxes, which will be charged (if applicable) based on your state or country of residence. Canadian residents will be charged applicable taxes. Offer not valid in Quebec. This offer is limited to one order per household. Books received may not be as shown. Not valid for current subscribers to the Harlequin Special Edition or Harlequin Heartwarming series. All orders subject to approval. Credit or debit balances in a customer's account(s) may be offset by any other outstanding balance owed by or to the customer. Please allow 4 to 6 weeks for delivery. Offer available while quantities last.

Your Privacy—Your information is being collected by Harlequin Enterprises ULC, operating as Harlequin Reader Service. For a complete summary of the information we collect, how we use this information and to whom it is disclosed, please visit our privacy notice located at corporate.harlequin.com/privacy-notice. From time to time we may also exchange your personal information with reputable third parties. If you wish to opt out of this sharing of your personal information, please visit readerservice.com/consumerschoice or call 1-800-873-8635. **Notice to California Residents**—Under California law, you have specific rights to control and access your data. For more information on these rights and how to exercise them, visit corporate.harlequin.com/california-privacy.

HSEHW22R2

Get 4 FREE REWARDS!

We'll send you 2 FREE Books plus 2 FREE Mystery Gifts.

FREE Value Over $20

Both the **Romance** and **Suspense** collections feature compelling novels written by many of today's bestselling authors.

YES! Please send me 2 FREE novels from the Essential Romance or Essential Suspense Collection and my 2 FREE gifts (gifts are worth about $10 retail). After receiving them, if I don't wish to receive any more books, I can return the shipping statement marked "cancel." If I don't cancel, I will receive 4 brand-new novels every month and be billed just $7.24 each in the U.S. or $7.49 each in Canada. That's a savings of up to 38% off the cover price. It's quite a bargain! Shipping and handling is just 50¢ per book in the U.S. and $1.25 per book in Canada.* I understand that accepting the 2 free books and gifts places me under no obligation to buy anything. I can always return a shipment and cancel at any time by calling the number below. The free books and gifts are mine to keep no matter what I decide.

Choose one: ☐ **Essential Romance**   ☐ **Essential Suspense**
                      (194/394 MDN GQ6M)   (191/391 MDN GQ6M)

Name (please print)

Address   Apt. #

City   State/Province   Zip/Postal Code

Email: Please check this box ☐ if you would like to receive newsletters and promotional emails from Harlequin Enterprises ULC and its affiliates. You can unsubscribe anytime.

Mail to the **Harlequin Reader Service:**
IN U.S.A.: P.O. Box 1341, Buffalo, NY 14240-8531
IN CANADA: P.O. Box 603, Fort Erie, Ontario L2A 5X3

Want to try 2 free books from another series? Call 1-800-873-8635 or visit www.ReaderService.com.

---

*Terms and prices subject to change without notice. Prices do not include sales taxes, which will be charged (if applicable) based on your state or country of residence. Canadian residents will be charged applicable taxes. Offer not valid in Quebec. This offer is limited to one order per household. Books received may not be as shown. Not valid for current subscribers to the Essential Romance or Essential Suspense Collection. All orders subject to approval. Credit or debit balances in a customer's account(s) may be offset by any other outstanding balance owed by or to the customer. Please allow 4 to 6 weeks for delivery. Offer available while quantities last.

Your Privacy—Your information is being collected by Harlequin Enterprises ULC, operating as Harlequin Reader Service. For a complete summary of the information we collect, how we use this information and to whom it is disclosed, please visit our privacy notice located at corporate.harlequin.com/privacy-notice. From time to time we may also exchange your personal information with reputable third parties. If you wish to opt out of this sharing of your personal information, please visit readerservice.com/consumerschoice or call 1-800-873-8635. **Notice to California Residents**—Under California law, you have specific rights to control and access your data. For more information on these rights and how to exercise them, visit corporate.harlequin.com/california-privacy.

STRS22R2